THE

GLACE BAY

MINERS'

MUSEUM

THE NOVEL

THE GLACE BAY MINERS' MUSEUM

THE NOVEL

BY SHELDON CURRIE

BRETON BOOKS
WRECK COVE, CAPE BRETON ISLAND
1995

This is the first publication of Sheldon Currie's novel, *The Glace Bay Miners' Museum*. Sheldon Currie's short story with the same title first appeared in *The Antigonish Review* (editor, Fr. R.J. MacSween), and then in the 1979 collection of Sheldon's stories, published under the same title by Bill Tierney at Deluge Press, Montreal. The story has also appeared in several anthologies, and was the basis of a CBC radio play by Wendy Lill.

Jerry Wexler read the story and fought for the next five years to get someone to take it seriously for film. Sheldon went on to write the present novel, itself a contribution toward Jerry Wexler and Mort Rancen's script for "The Glace Bay Miners' Museum," the working title for the new motion picture directed by Mort Rancen and produced by Ranfilm Productions Inc., Imagex, Les Productions Télé-Action Inc., and Skyline Productions.

Breton Books Editor: Ronald Caplan
Production Assistant: Bonnie Thompson

Canadian Cataloguing in Publication Data
Currie, Sheldon.

The Glace Bay Miners' Museum

ISBN 1-895415-05-5

I. Title.

PS8555.U74G52 1994   C813'.54   C95-950028-6
PR9199.3.C82G52 1994

"Margaret, are you grieving?..."

from *Spring and Fall*
by Gerard Manley Hopkins

CONTENTS

Chapter One

The White Rose Café

THE FIRST TIME I ever saw the bugger, I thought to myself, him as big as he is, me as small as I am, if he was astraddle on the road, naked, I could walk under him without a hair touching. That's the thought I had; he was coming down the aisle of the White Rose Café, looking to the right and looking to the left at the people in the booths. The size of him would kill you, so everybody was looking at him. I was looking at him too because I knew all the booths were full except mine. I was sitting in the last one, my back to the kitchen, so I could see everybody coming and going. He had a box in his hand, looked like a tool box, and I was wondering if he'd sit with me and show me what was in his box. I made a dollar keeping house for MacDonalds and came to the Bay to spend it on tea and chips and sit in the restaurant and watch the goings on. The going on was the same old thing: girls sitting with boys and boys sitting with girls, trying to pair off to suit themselves, and making a cup of tea and chips last as long as they could so they wouldn't have to leave. It was hard to find somebody on the street. You could go to the show and sit in the dark and hope somebody would sit next to you and hold your hand, but that cost money too, and hardly ever worked. It worked once for me, this fella sat beside me and I knew it was a chance because the theatre was almost empty. I figured he saw my hair before the lights went out. I had this lovely long hair. I was lucky enough, I bought a nut bar on the way in and I gave him a piece. He took my hand. He had a huge hand. Pan shovel hands we used to call people with hands like that. We used to think you got them from loading coal with a pan shovel. My hand disappeared in his in the dark. He put his big hand on top of my knees which I was keeping together. It felt like he had taken my hand off at the wrist and moved it up to my knee. I couldn't see it and for a minute I couldn't feel it and I was sitting there looking at his big mitt and wondering if my hand was still in it. Then it started to sweat and I could feel it again. We stayed like that through two shows. We never said a word. When we came out we walked down to Senator's Corner and down Commercial Street to Eaton's where the buses stopped. We never said a word. We stood next to each other and I stared at the Medical Hall and he stared at Thompson and Sutherland. Then the bus came for Number 11 and he got on. He didn't even look out the window at me.

I was sitting alone in the White Rose because none of the boys would sit with me and none of the girls would because the boys wouldn't. For one thing I had a runny nose. They called me names and if a boy went with me they called him names. George MacNeil walked home with me from school one day—it was on the way to his house anyway— and I heard in the cloakroom next day—they had a vent between the boys' cloakroom and the girls'—I heard somebody from another class say to him, "I see you're taking out snotface these days. Don't forget to kiss her on the back of her head."

For another thing I screwed a couple of boys when I

3

was a little girl. I didn't know you weren't supposed to, but I didn't want to anyway, and I wouldn't but this fella offered me a nickel and I never had a nickel. Then he asked if I'd do it with his cousin and I said no. But then he came to me himself, the cousin, and told me he went to the washhouse every Saturday his father was on day shift for five times and waited for him to come up and waited for him to shower and followed him to the pay office and asked him for a dime, and had to promise to cut enough sticks for the week. I found out later he sold two quarts of blueberries that he stole, but he wanted to tell me a nice long story. Anyway I felt sorry for him, and he had fifty cents. So he told me to meet him up in the woods by the Scotchtown road between the bootleg pits and Rabbit Town. I didn't know then that he didn't want to walk up there with me. Anyway, I didn't really screw either one of them because they didn't know how to do it and it was too late before I could tell them, although, God knows, I knew little enough myself of the little there is to know. They didn't walk home with me either, neither one. But they told everybody I was a whore. So I was not only a whore, but a snot-nosed whore. You could hardly blame the boys and girls for not sitting with me.

So I was sitting alone in the last booth at the White Rose Café when this giant of a man with a box in his hand came bearing down the aisle looking left and right, and he kept on coming until he got to my booth and saw there was nobody there but me. I remember it seemed like it got darker when he stood in front of me, he blacked out so much light with the size of him. He had on a big lumberjack shirt. I thought, when he stood there holding his box, before he said anything, I said to myself, I wish he'd pick me up and put me in his shirt pocket.

"Can I put this here on your table?" he said; he pointed his chin at his box.

"Suit yourself," I said to him awful loud. He was so big, I thought I had to yell for him to hear me.

"Can I sit down, then?" he said.

"Suit yourself again," I said. So he put his box on the table and sat down opposite me, and I could feel his knees about an inch from mine. I could feel the heat coming from his knees. I could have exploded I was so happy. But I kept my lips tight.

The waitress pounced on us right away. "Hi, snooker," she said. She was dying to find out who this fella was. So was everybody in the restaurant. I could see the ones facing me. I could feel the ones not facing me wishing they had sat on the other side of the booth. Nobody knew who he was. I just wanted to know what he had in the box.

"Something?" Kitten said, and looked at me and looked at him.

"I had something," I said.

"Would you have something else?" the man said. "I'd like to buy you a bite to eat if you don't mind." I near died. That was the first polite thing anybody ever said to me since my father got killed.

"I don't mind if I do," I said.

"Well, what is it then?" Kitten said. "What you want?"

"I'll have a cup of tea and an order of chips," I said.

"Will you now?" Kitten said.

"Yes," I said. "I will."

"I'll have the same," the man with the box said.

"Thank you," Kitten said, and wrote it down, saying very slowly to herself like she was talking to a baby: Two orders of chips and two orders of tea. "That will be fine," she said, looking at me and looking at him. "I'll go see if we got any."

She went away and I looked at my little hands and I could feel my knees getting warmer and warmer. I couldn't think of anything to say. My back was cold and I thought I might start to shake if I didn't talk, but I couldn't think of anything. I looked up at him and he was looking at his hands. He had a lot to look at. Nobody said a word till Kitten came back. "Here you are," she said, "two teas and two chips. Medium rare."

We ate a few chips and took the bags out of our teas and put them in the ash tray. Then he said: "Well, what do you think?"

"I think you're the biggest son of a bitch I ever saw," I said.

7

He looked at me then when I said that, as if I just came in, and the look of him made me feel as if I just came in. I felt my back get warm, and I leant back against the back of the booth. He started to laugh. He must of laughed for two minutes but it seemed to me two days, and it sounded like somebody playing some kind of instrument I never heard before. When he stopped, he said, "Know what I think?"

"What?" I said.

"I think you're the smallest son of a bitch I ever saw."

Then we both of us laughed for two minutes. Then we talked about the weather as if nothing happened, but I could feel the heat on my knees. After a while he said: "Well now. What's your name?"

"Margaret MacNeil."

"Well now, Miss MacNeil. It's been a pleasure meeting you. Do you come here often?"

"Every week at this same exact time," I said.

"Very well then," he said. "Perhaps we'll meet again. What do you think?"

"Suit yourself," I said.

"O.K.," he said, "I will. My name is Neil Currie."

Then he got up and opened the box.

When he got the box open it was full of brown sticks and a plaid bag. Bagpipes! I never seen bagpipes before. Never knew there was any. Never heard them before. God only knows I heard them enough since. He pulled it all out of the box and started putting sticks on sticks till it was together; then he pumped it up. It snarled a couple of times, then when he had it between his arm and his ribs he came down on it with his elbow and it started to squeal, and everybody in the café either leaned out or stood up to look at the God-awful racket.

Then his fingers started jumping and it started playing something I don't know what it was. To me it sounded like a cut cat jumping from table to table and screaming like a tiger. Before you knew it the Chinaman came from the front. He didn't stop, he just slowed down to squeeze by the man and the pipes. When he got through he walked backwards a minute toward the kitchen and yelled: "Get that goddam fiddle out of here." Then two big Chinamen came out of the kitchen; I always thought Chinamen were small until I saw them two. They each had a hand of cards like

9

they were playing cards and kept their hands so nobody could peek at them while they were out. They were just as big as Neil was, maybe bigger, and you never saw how fast two men can put one man and an armload of bagpipes out of a restaurant and into the street.

I went out after him. I took him out his box. I passed the Chinamen coming back in. They didn't do nothing to him, just fired him to the street and went back with their cards. He was sitting on the street. I helped him stuff his bagpipes in his box. Then he stood up and took the box in his hand. He looked down at me and he said, "One thing I thought a Chinaman would never have the nerve to do is criticize another man's music. If I wasn't drunk, I'd give you my pipes to hold and I'd go back in there and get the shit kicked out of me."

"Where do you live?" I said.

"I have a room down on Brookside."

"Want me to walk down?"

"Where do you live?"

"I live in Reserve."

"Let's get the bus, then. I'll see you home. Sober me

up. Perhaps you could make us a cup of tea."

"O.K.," I said.

"You live with your father and mother?"

"I live with my mother and grandfather. My father got killed in the pit. Come on. It's starting to rain. My brother too."

The rain banged on the roof of the bus all the way to Reserve and when we got off it was pouring and muddy all the way up to the shack where we lived. My father built it himself because, he said, he never would live in a company house. He had to work in the goddamn company mine, but he didn't have to live in the goddamn company house, with god only knows who in the next half. My mother said he was too mean to pay rent, but only when he wasn't around did she say it. She only said it once to his face. But he got killed.

It was dark even though it was only after seven. It was October. We had to take off our shoes and ring out our socks from walking in puddles up the lane. We didn't have a real road in. Just a track where they came with groceries and coal. We hung them down the side of the scuttle and

11

our jackets on the oven door. "I'll get you an old pair of Daddy's pants soon's Mama gets out of the bedroom. You're the first one I ever saw could fit."

"You're right on time, Marg," Mama said. "I think I'll run up the Hall. Who you got here?"

"You'll get soaked."

"I know, but I better go. I might win the thousand."

"This is Neil Currie."

"Where'd you find him?"

"In the Bay."

"Are you from the Bay?"

"No. I just came."

"Where from?"

"St. Andrew's Channel."

"Never heard of that. You working in the pit?"

"I was. I started but I got fired."

"You look like you could shovel. Why'd they fire you?"

"I wouldn't talk English to the foreman."

"You an Eyetalian?"

"No."

"Well, I have to run or I'll be late. Don't forget your

grandfather, Margie. I hit him about an hour ago so he's about ready."

"O.K. Mom. Hope you win it."

"Me too."

That was my mother's joke; about hitting my grandfather. Anytime a stranger was in she said it. He had something wrong with his lungs. Every hour or two he couldn't breathe and we'd have to pound him on the chest. So somebody had to be in the house every minute. When Mama left I got Neil the pants. "You might as well keep them," I said. "They won't fit nobody else ever comes around here." Then I went in to change my dress.

I expected to be a while because I wanted to fix myself up on my mother's make-up. It was her room, though I had to sleep in it, and she had a lot of stuff for make-up. My brother slept in the other room with my grandfather. We just had the three. Where you come in was the kitchen and that's where you were if you weren't in the bedroom or in the cellar getting potatoes. But I didn't stay to fix up because I just got my dress half on when he started wailing on his bag and pipes.

I stuck my head out the door. "Are you out of your brain?" I yelled but he couldn't hear with the noise. So I got my dress all on and went out and put my hands over two of the holes the noise came out. They have three holes. He stopped. "My grandfather," I said, "you'll wake him up." I no sooner said it when the knock came. "There he is now," I said. "I'm sorry," he said. "I forgot your grandfather."

"It's O.K.," I said. "I think it must be time for his hit now anyway." I went in and I got the surprise of my life.

He could talk, my grandfather, but he didn't. It hurt him to talk after he came back from the hospital once with his lungs and he quit. I don't know if it got better or not because he never tried again; same as he quit walking after he got out of breath once from it. He took to writing notes. He had a scribbler and a pencil by him and he wrote what he wanted: "Thump me chest; dinner; beer; water; piss pot; did she win; did you pay the lite bill; then put on the lites; piece of bread; ask the priest to come; time to go now father; I have to get me thump. No, Ian'll do it." See, that's just one page. He had a whole stack of scribblers after a while. They're all here. We have them numbered.

14

So I went in, and I was after sitting him up in place to do his thump; you had to put him in a certain way. And he started to bang his long finger on the scribbler he had in his hand.

"Tell him to play."

"Well, Christ in harness," I said, which is what my grandfather used to say when he talked and now I always said it to tease him. "Watch your tongue," he wrote me one day. "Somebody got to say it now you're dumb," I said. "If I don't it won't get said."

"Do you want your thump?" I said and he wrote in his scribbler, "No, tell him to play." So I told Neil to play. "Isn't that lovely?" Neil said and laughed. And he played. It sounded to me like two happy hens fighting over a bean, and when he stopped and asked me if I knew what tune it was I told him what it sounded like to me and he laughed and laughed.

"Do you like the tune?"

"It's not too bad."

"Would you see if your grandfather liked it?" So I went. And he was sound asleep with his scribbler in his

15

hands on his belly. He wrote on it: "When he comes back ask him if he can play these." And he had a list I couldn't read. Here it is here in the scribbler:

Guma slan to na ferriv chy harish achune
Va me nday Ben Doran
Bodichin a Virun
Falte go ferrin ar balech in eysgich

I took the scribbler out and showed it to Neil and he said he would. "I'll have to practice a little."

"Play some more now," I asked him. "Play that one again."

"What one?"

"The one you put him to sleep with."

"'Mairi's Wedding.'"

"Yes."

"About the bean and the chickens."

"Yes."

So he played. I was getting interested in it. My foot started tapping and my knees which I had been holding together all night fell. As soon as he saw that, I was sitting on a chair against the wall, he came over and came down to kiss me. I put my two feet on his chest and pushed. I was hoping to fire him across the room but nothing happened. It kept him off, but he just stayed there with his chest on my feet looking up my leg and me with a hole in my underwear.

"What's the matter with you?" he said.

I said, "Just because you play that thing, don't mean you can jump me." He ran his hand down my leg and nearly drove me nuts.

"Fuck off," I said. I thought that would shock him back but he just stayed there leaning against my sneakers. He tried to take my hand but I just put the two of them behind the chair.

"I won't jump you till we're married," he said.

"Married?" I said. "Who'd marry you? You're nothing but a goddamn Currie." Then he started laughing and moved back.

"And why wouldn't you marry a goddamn Currie?" he said.

"Because they just come in your house, play a few snarls on their pipes and they think you'll marry them for that."

"Well, well, well," he said. "I'll tell you what. I'll play

for you every night till you're ready. And I'll make you a song of your own."

"What kind of song?"

"I don't know, we'll wait and see what I can make."

"Well, well, well," I said. "I want a song a person can sing so I'll be sure what it's saying."

"O.K., I'll make you two. One to sing and one to guess at."

"Good," I said. "If I like them, well, who knows what might happen."

"What would you like for the singing one?"

"I don't know."

"Well, what's the happiest thing in your life or the saddest?"

"They're both the same," I said. "My brother. Not the one living here now but my older brother, Charlie. We called him Charlie Dave, though Dave was my father's name. That was to tell him from the other Charlie Mac-Neils. There's quite a few around here. Charlie Pig, and Charlie Spider. And a lot more. Charlie Big Dan. I really liked Charlie Dave."

"What happened to him?"

"He got killed in the pit with my father."

"How old was he?"

"He was just sixteen. He used to fight for me. Wouldn't let anybody call me names."

"He mustn't have been in the pit very long?"

"Not even a year. He started working with my grandfather just before he had to quit for his lungs. Then he started with my father. Then he was killed. They were both killed. He was good in school too, but he got married so he had to work. They didn't even have a chance to have their baby."

"What happened to his wife?"

"Oh, she's still around. She's nice. She had her baby. A sweet baby. They live up in the Rows. In a company house. With her mother and her sister." I started to cry then so I made a cup of tea.

SO AFTER THAT he came back every night and it was nothing but noise. My mother took to going out every night. When I told her he asked me to get married, she said:

"That man will never live in a company house. You'll be moving out of one shack and into another."

"I can stand it," I said.

"You can stand it," she said. "You can stand it. And is he going to work?"

"He's going to look up at Number 10."

"Good," she said. "He can work with Ian. They can die together. And you can stand it. And you can live in your shack alone. Stand it, then."

The first night, after he played one of the songs my grandfather asked him, he played one he said he made for me. I loved it. It made me grin, so I kept my head down and I held my knees together with my arms.

"What's the name of it?" I asked.

"The name of it is 'Two Happy Beans Fighting Over a Chicken.'"

"Go whan," I said.

"Do you like it?"

"Not bad. What's the real name?"

"'Margaret's Wedding,'" he said.

"Christ in harness." I almost let go my knees.

20

The next night he played it again and he played another one for my grandfather.

Then we went up the Haulage Road to Number 10 to get Ian. I always went to walk home with him because when he started he was scared when he was night shift to come home alone in the dark. I kept on ever since. Sometimes he had a girl friend would go. I never asked him if he stopped being scared. He never often had to try it alone. He didn't come home that night, he decided to work a double shift. So we walked back alone that night, but we took to going up together for Ian when he was night shift till Neil got the job there too and they were buddies in the pit so they worked the same shifts and came home together till we got married and moved to the Bay.

They fought like two mongrels. Miners said they never saw two men enjoy their work so much because it kept them close enough so they could fight every minute. Then on Sunday afternoon they came to our home and they sat in the kitchen and drank rum and played forty-five and fought and fought and fought.

What they fought about was politics and religion, or

so they said. Ian would tell Neil that the only hope for the miner was to vote in a labour government.

"How are you going to manage that?"

"By voting. Organizing."

"When is that going to happen?"

"We have to work for it."

"The future?"

"Yes, the future."

"There's no future," Neil would say.

"There has to be a future."

"See in the bedroom, Ian. See your grandfather. That's the future."

"Well, he's there. The future is there."

"He's there all right. He can't breathe, he can't talk, he can't walk. You know the only thing he's got? Some old songs in his head, that he can hardly remember, that your father hardly even knew and you don't know at all. Came here and lost their tongues, their music, their songs. Everything but their shovels."

"Too bad you wouldn't lose yours. Have a drink and shut up."

"I will not shut up. However, I will have a drink."

He seemed so drunk to me I thought it'd spill out his mouth if he took more; but he took it. "Nothing left," he said. "Nothing. Only thing you can do different from a pit pony is drink rum and play forty-five."

Ian pointed to the cat curled up on the wood box. "Look, it's almost seven o'clock," he said. "Why don't you take that tomcat and go to Benediction since you like to sing so much. Then you can sing with him tonight. Out in the bushes. He goes out same time as you leave."

"What are you talking about?"

"You're buddies. You and the cat. You can sing near as good as he can. He's near fond of religion as you are."

"All I can say," Neil said, "is pit ponies can't go to church."

"Is that all you can say?" Ian said. "Well, all I can say is, if a pit pony went to church, that would do him some lot of good."

"Ian, you do not understand what I am talking about."

"That is the God's truth for you, Neil. Now why don't

you go on the couch and have a lay down."

And that's the way Sunday afternoon and evening went. We could've been out for a walk, just as easy, and more fun.

But that second night that he came we walked down the Haulage Road, pitch black, and he sang me the song I asked him for about my brother. He sang it over and over till I knew it by heart. He sang it to me. "That's lovely," I told him.

I took him by the arm behind his elbow and slowed him down till he stopped and turned. I was crying but I told him anyway. "I'm going to get married to you." We kissed each other. Salt water was all over our lips. I think he must have been crying too. I wrote the song down in one of my grandfather's scribblers when we got back. Here it is here in this one here.

> *My brother was a miner*
> *His name was Charlie David*
> *He spent his young life laughing*
> *And digging out his grave.*
>
> *Charlie Dave was big*
> *Charlie Dave was strong*

Charlie Dave was two feet wide
And almost six feet long.

When Charlie David was sixteen
He learned to chew and spit
And went one day with Grandpa
To work down in the pit.   (chorus)

When Charlie David was sixteen
He met his Maggie June
On day shift week they met at eight
On back shift week at noon.   (chorus)

When Charlie David was sixteen
He said to June "Let's wed"
Maggie June was so surprised
She fell right out of bed.   (chorus)

When Charlie David was sixteen
They had a little boy
Maggie June was not surprised
Charlie danced for joy.   (chorus)

When Charlie David was sixteen
The roof fell on his head
His laughing mouth is full of coal
Charlie Dave is dead.

The next night when he came I told him I had to pay him back for his songs. I'd tell him a story.

"O.K.," he said. "Tell me a story."

"This is a true story."

"That's the kind I like," he said.

"O.K. There was this fella worked in the pit, his name was George Stepenak, he was a Pole, they eat all kinds of stuff, took garlic in his can, used to stink. His can would stink and his breath would stink. The men used to tease him all the time, which made him cross. One day my father said:

"'George, what in the name of Jesus have you got in your can?'

"'Shit,' George said to my father.

"'I know that,' my father said. 'But what you put on it to make it smell so bad?'"

When my grandfather found out I told him a story to pay him back for the song, he wanted to tell him one. He wrote it out for him in a scribbler. Here it is here. Well, he didn't write it all out, he just wrote it out for me to tell it.

"Tell about Jonny and Angie loading in 24, the roof so low they hadda take pancakes in their cans."

That's the way it went from then on. Every night he'd come and play and sing. Me and my grandfather would tell or write stories. My brother even would try to sing when he was on day shift or back shift. But he worked a lot of night shift. That's the way it went till Neil got work. When he got work we got married as soon as he built this house. Soon as he got the job he said: "I got some land on North Street. I'll build a house before we get married. It's right on the ocean. You can hear the waves." And he did. He did. And you can see, it's no shack. He must of been a carpenter. Soon as the house was finished, we got married and moved in. Him and my brother Ian were buddies by then, working the same shifts. And when they weren't working they were at our place arguing or playing cards. That's one way Ian was like me. He loved to play cards.

Chapter Two

The Card Game and the Mine Accident

I LOVE TO PLAY CARDS. The only thing is whenever I sat to play it always brought me back to the night Dad and Charlie Dave got killed. I was playing cards that night. I was up at the underground manager's house helping my mother with her job at housecleaning and I got in a game of cards with the girls, me and Mary against Morag and Minnie, so I stayed on and played and Mother went home. I could feel it in my bones when the phone rang but even before that I could see it in the cards. All them shovels. I knew it when I saw all the spades. Not right away. First I thought I was lucky. The five, the king, the queen, the jack and the ten of spades. I had all the big ones except the aces. I hoped my partner would have at least one and maybe a few back-up cards, but when I bid 30 for 60 in spades Mary threw in all her five cards.

I loved to play cards. I loved to because it was exciting to be winning, or losing and trying not to. But when it was over even if you lost you didn't seem to lose anything. Everybody still had on all their clothes, all their money, if they had any, the cards all went back to the pack, and it seemed like fair to everybody, unless somebody cheated, and even then they'd get caught, likely. Even marbles, if you lost you'd lose your marbles, and even if I won, which I usually did, I'd feel sorry for the other person who'd have no marbles left to play with, especially if I cheated. It'd take the shine off winning. But I only cheated against boys, because they always beat me by cheating, or bullying, or just plain stealing, picking up my marbles and walking off, and laughing me off if I went after them. Mostly I'd play with them only if Charlie Dave was with me. They only tried it once with him there. That was a sight to behold, I'll tell ya. I never in my life saw the like of it, except in movies, you know, where they have three galoots in black hats picking on a widow, or a cripple, or just some poor cowboy having a quiet drink in a saloon after a hard month's work, or getting cheated at at cards, and in walks the white hat and bang, bang, bang, end of the evening. That was Charlie Dave.

I was playing with this Greg Campbell. All the marbles were out. He had borrowed quite a few from his buddies when I got ahead and everything they owned was out there or already in my bag. I had the last knock, but I had a hard shot because the way we were playing I had to tell which of his marbles I was going for, then I'd knock one against the building so it would fly back and land near that marble I was after, or kiss it. If it kissed it, I won everything on the ground, if it didn't I had to span the distance between them with my hand from thumb to little finger. If I could I got everything on the ground, and if I couldn't and he could span with two hands then he got everything. If not, it was his turn. That time I got a kissey. It wasn't just luck. They thought I was lucky, but I practiced, and I practiced against a wall where I usually played; in fact I usually wouldn't play except against a wall I practiced at, so I knew the wall and I knew the ground and I used my killer marble that I saved for such times. I never lost with that marble. I practiced with it every day. When he saw my kissey he grabbed most of the marbles and his two buddies grabbed the rest and they walked off. Charlie Dave was on him like a cat. He grabbed him by the scruff of the neck and planked him on the ground on his back, broke open his hands and spilled all the marbles all over the ground before the other two came at him. He kicked the first one on the chin when he came at him running low, and he kicked the next one in the nuts. And that was it. The three of them on the ground looking like they were trying to wake up for school. I went over and took the marbles out of their pockets. Of course he had to be the one got killed in the pit. Them three Campbells, they'll likely live to a hundred. They're still going strong, and still stunned galoots.

I loved to play cards too because it got me out. And you could play with grown-up people, and even beat them without them letting you. I played cribbage all the time with my grandfather. He loved it because there wasn't much else he could do except write in his scribblers. He never let me win. He wrote down in his scribbler, "If you win from me you know you won." That was why I liked to play with him. But I really liked to get out. Even people who didn't want to be friends with me in public I could have fun with in their houses playing cards. If nothing else their parents made them be half-decent to me. Of course they were never allowed to come to my house. But I had to put up with that.

I learned to love cards when I was little. My mother would tell our fortunes. She couldn't play cards for beans, but she could tell fortunes. She could keep you going for an hour on the edge of your chair with all the amazing things that might happen to you. People would come to the house just to have her do it, and she'd often stay after bingo and do it for her bingo friends. Everybody told her she should charge and make a little money out of it, but she always would say, "Sure, so people would take me for a goddamn gypsy. It's bad enough as it is."

So first I thought I was lucky when I saw all the high spades. But then I thought of my mother.

"Spades are death," she said. "Shovels dig the hole. The only thing can save you is a heart. A heart can block four shovels."

"Why is that?" I said.

"Isn't it obvious?" she said. "The heart means desire.

Only heart's desire can conquer, even death." I think my mother thought she was teaching us to be happy and expect the best. And you do get happy sometimes, but what do you do when death conquers the heart? My mother could never face that. To her the answer for everything was bingo. Her father always called her "my little groyoch" which she thought was a pet name, and always smiled when he said it to her, she didn't know a lick of Gaelic. When she heard people speak it she thought they were Eyetalians, and her father couldn't speak a word of English till he went to school. What it really means in English is "my little pain in the arse." That's what my grandfather told me. Another time I asked him what a groyoch is he said it's like a cow that gives a whole bucketful of beautiful, creamy milk, morning and night, but every time with the last spurt she puts her shitty hoof in the bucket.

Yes, first I thought I was lucky when I saw the high spades, but then I thought of my mother. And then I re-membered the dogs howling every night for the past three nights at the full moon, those goddamn dogs, once one starts, they all start.

With four playing auction forty-five, you know there are twenty-four cards out including the kitty, that's nearly half the cards. I was dealing. Minnie took four cards, my partner Mary took five, Morag took three, which made thirty-six cards out, which left sixteen cards in the deck. I figured both aces were out, but who knows. I looked at Mary as if to say blink if you got one, blink twice if you got two, but she stared wide-eyed. I figured she didn't have them because she'd rather cheat than eat. The other two were humming "I lost my heart in a highland glen" but I couldn't go by that because one of them might have given a contrary sign which would mean she really had what she was singing she didn't have, the ace of hearts.

Anyway if the aces were still out I had a chance of picking one up and I really wanted that ace of hearts so I threw away the ten of spades, which was taking a chance, because if the aces were still in the deck and stayed there, I had a big chance of winning with the ten especially if my partner had anything half-decent. But I wanted that ace of hearts. I wanted to spoil that flush of deadly spades. So I threw in the ten and dealt myself the card off the top of the deck

I picked up the hand and looked. The five, the king, the queen, the jack, and there it was, the ace of spades.

I said to myself it doesn't mean a thing. It's only cards. Once my mother told me my fortune, this was when I half believed in her nonsense, and she said, "You're going to go on a trip by yourself. You will suffer, but when the pain is gone you will meet a tall dark stranger and you will be happy." The next week I went to the dentist and he nearly pulled my jaw off and on the tram car by myself, and the conductor, a tall dark stranger, my mother's second cousin I found out later, talked to me all the way home and let me drive the tram, sitting on his knee when there was no other passengers on. *Well I guess* I was happy. I was happy enough to get out of the house let alone drive the tram car. He made me promise not to tell anybody he let me do it. That made it even better. It was the biggest secret I had that year. It almost burst me. My mother made the appointment at the dentist but didn't tell me about it till a week after she told my fortune. She never fooled me again after that.

So I put my mind on winning the game. The only way I could lose was if someone had the ace of hearts and two spades to slough off on my five and jack. If my partner could take the first trick and lead a spade, then only Minnie on my left could beat us if she had the ace of hearts. I blinked at Mary and she blinked back twice meaning she had at least two spades and so she won the first trick, she could lead a trump. She might even have the ace of hearts, but she couldn't tell me any more, they were watching her like a hawk. She could sing a heart song, but then when we won they'd just say we cheated. You really only should cheat at the first half of the hand. I got excited planning it out and then the siren started to wail.

Minnie and Mary and Morag, their father was the underground manager. He was working the night shift. My father and Charlie Dave worked for him. They had the telephone. We all put down our cards. We all had the same thought. Should we run to the pit, or wait for the telephone to ring. We sat there. And waited. Their mother Margaret waited in the kitchen by the telephone. We could hear her waiting. She had a bad hip, she couldn't walk to the pit let alone run, so she had to wait.

Mother told them not to go to work that day.

"I suppose you saw it in the cards," Dada said to her. He was only joking, but she hard-faced him even though she knew he was joking, she let on he was criticising.

"Never mind the cards," she said. "I know you think everything I do is foolish. You know goddamn well lots of miners stay home the last day before the vacation for fear they'll get killed or hurt and ruin their vacation and everybody else's, because it never fails something happens on the last day."

"Well, it failed last year," Dada said. "Nobody was hurt last year."

"Oh, yes," she said, "What about that George Smith fella in West Virginia." I knew she was making that up because he had her in a corner, but if he thought so he didn't say. He just said: "You're in the wrong country, girl, this is Cape Breton, not the United States of America. No Cape Breton miner was hurt last year, day before vacation. Or week before. Or month before. They were only twelve men hurt last year and only three of them killed, because I went to three funerals, and I went to the hospital nine times. And they all happened before Christmas."

"That does not mean they weren't supposed to," she said, her eyes going harder and tightening her lips. She gave up the talk about Virginia right away, so then I knew for sure she made it up. "It may be," she said, "that the reason nobody was hurt is that he didn't go to work, so he couldn't get killed in the pit, if he was at work in his garden."

"I can make more money today in the pit," Dada said, "than I can save on vegetables if I work every day of the vacation in the garden."

"Oh. Yes. Indeed you can. Yes. Indeed you can. And we know what today's money is for, don't we? If you spent today in the garden, and the next two weeks in the garden, instead of today in the pit and the next two weeks drinking, then you'd have more money at the end of it, and vegetables too. And not rumsick too at the end of it."

Through all this Charlie Dave stood with his lunch can under his arm, and a smirk on his face. She looked at him finally and her face softened. "This I know for sure," she said, you could see the tears starting, and you could hear them in her throat. "If you don't go to the pit today, you won't get killed in it, and I'll buy you the moonshine myself." And the two of them pursed their lips, and lifted their hands like in a little wave, and out the door, and out the world altogether. Never to be laid eyes on again.

When the telephone rang we shot to the kitchen. It wasn't their ring but of course Maggie picked it up, everybody would be on it and somebody might have the news. They had thirteen on the line so maybe whoever was calling had the news for whoever was the unlucky family or maybe it was just somebody who found out calling a friend, but they'd know everybody was listening so who knows how much they'd tell. We never found out because Maggie put it to her ear and listened a minute, and let out a little squeal like a little pig, and sank down the wall to the floor, fainted or dead, we didn't know. Morag picked up the phone and listened and said, "There's nobody on it," she said, and then said, "Hello... hello... HELLO, *HELLO*, HELLO, hello."

We hit the road for the pit. It was windy as the beach, the wind blowing our dresses between our legs blowing us back. We got there, puffed out, and half of Reserve there ahead of us, some of them even in their underwear, and coal black faced miners everywhere, it was a pitch black night, you could see their clothes better than their faces, except for their staring eyes, some of them had their lanterns on their hats still on and you couldn't see them but they could see you. And everybody was walking around and asking who was hurt, was anybody killed, are they up yet. The ambulance was waiting where the trip comes up and we could hear the noises of something coming up, and up came a boxcar and a bunch of men got out. I saw one I knew and I grabbed his arm and asked him, "Who's hurt, Johnnie?" and he wouldn't look at me, he set his eyes over my head and stared, and he wouldn't talk, he hung open his mouth and shook his head back and forth, and then the trip came up again with two men and a stretcher on it and I streaked for it, but somebody grabbed me and carried me like a baby and said, "Your father and brother is hurt, Maggie, I'm taking you home." I twisted and squirmed, but I couldn't kick loose, and then I just sank and cried.

He carried me all the way home, telling me to say my prayers, and he was saying our fathers and hail marys and glory be to the fathers, just like he was saying the rosary. I didn't know who he **was,** but he was my Uncle Rory, who I never met before because my mother never went there because he was a moonshiner, she always said that we might not be big shots but at least we're not bootleggers. And my father always said, "Well, we might not be bootleggers, but we can handle the product." And she always said, "Well, that's the God's truth for you, nothing to brag about." She always let on she didn't drink. Of course she didn't compared to him. She'd always say, "Well, I'll have a hot one," which meant sugar and boiling water in the moonshine, which she pretended was more like medicine than a real drink.

As soon as he set me down on the step to open the door I streaked for the hospital. It was two or three miles but I cut that in half with short cuts. I went straight to the emergency, going through the ambulance door, I knew where it was from the time Grandfather was rushed there, nobody was there to stop me and I went right in, but my mother and her brother were there already, somebody must of drove them down, she was sitting on a bench, sobbing, or more like squeaking, with her head in her hands and bobbing her head up and down with every squeak. He had his arm around her, his face was black with coal dust, he was just staring at the three stretcher-beds, his eyes like lights shining out of his black face and without a blink of them at all, he waved me to sit beside him and when I did he put his arm around my shoulders too.

"Are they gonna be O.K.?" I said.

"No," he said, "they're not."

I put my head in my hands and cried. I bawled.

After I bawled, I sobbed for a while and then I said, "I'm going to look at them."

"Better not," my uncle said. But I went anyway. I pulled the sheet down off their faces. Their faces were black with coal dust and didn't look like anything was wrong with them except they were dirty. They both of them had smiles on their faces. I thought maybe one of them told a joke just before the two of them died and, pain and all, they both laughed and ended up with a smile. Probably not true but it made me feel good to think about it like that, and when the sister came in I asked her if I could clean their faces and she said, "No, certainly not," but I said, "Ah, c'mon, it's my brother and father, I want to," and she looked at me, and looked at me, and at last she said, "Of course, of course, I'll get some soap and water."

When she came back she helped me. Not doing it, but more like showing me how, and talking to me, saying things like this is a very handsome man, and you must have been very proud of your brother when I told her how Charlie Dave would fight for me, and you're lucky you have another brother; of course I was but Ian had nothing on Charlie Dave, but he was younger and might change, but she talked to me and made it all seem normal, the two of us standing over a dead face and cleaning the dirt off of it. The only other thing I remember a nun ever saying to me was, "Margaret, you get to your seat, this minute."

Chapter Three

The Wakes

EVEN THEN THEY HAD funeral homes, mostly for well-off people, and because we had two dead, and a small place, because the miners wouldn't let us pay for a thing, they bought the caskets and the flowers, and they dug the holes for us, some people expected we would wake them at the home, but even my mother didn't care how poor it made us look, she said no, "They're my men and they'll wake in my own house. David built this house, if you'd call it that, because he wouldn't live in a company house. Surely to God if he could live in it, small as it is, he can be dead in it. He built it for me is what he said, but I know who he built it for. He was a miner not a carpenter. He would have been handier at it if we wanted to live in a cave, and come to think of it, we might not be any the worse off." My mother was never satisfied with anything but mostly she was never satisfied with the house, and she never stopped complaining about it even after he was dead, even at the wake it was her favorite topic, outside of Charlie Dave, which was her favorite topic, but only in her head because every time she tried to talk about him she broke down sobbing.

The wake was so crowded it got to be more like a picnic than a wake. Everybody in Reserve came to that wake. Of course every miner came, they always did, no matter who was killed they came like it was a brother. Two people in the one family killed at the same time made it into a more important event I guess so a lot more came than expected. I never seen so many women in my life. A lot of people never came near the shacks, which is what they called where we lived, and some of the places were not much more than shacks, though our place was a lot better than a shack. My father was not a carpenter but he could still saw straight. So a lot of people took the chance of the wake to come down and see how we lived, and I think a lot were surprised at how nice some of the places were, although, still, some places were pretty bad.

A good thing it was the summer and not raining because most people had to be outside, there was hardly enough room in the house for the food and drink let alone people. They had to come in by two's to pay their respects, and the women, as soon as they got off the kneeling bench, they'd get up before their husbands and pretend to be waiting for them and try to wiggle their way into the kitchen to see what that was like, and my mother died a thousand deaths every time one of them managed it, not that there was anything wrong with the kitchen, but it was small and didn't have a pantry so it was crowded. Dada always promised to build on a pantry but he never got around to it. "Too busy dealing with demerara," my mother always said. She often did housework up Main Street for some families up there, and sometimes up on Official Row, or Reserve Rows, and every time she'd come home she'd be saying, "Now, if I had a kitchen like that...."

Every woman that came brought food, a lot of people then still had gardens and pigpens and chickens, and some who lived a little out who had pastures would have a cow, and a good thing they did, we had to feed everybody, but we ended up with too much and had to give it away. We had an icebox but it would only hold so much and it wasn't that easy to get the ice in July. Hams and chickens. We could of started a butcher shop. We kept the hams, they were smoked and would keep in the cellar, but everybody in a mile of us had chicken for supper for a week.

We had our couch in the living room because our kitchen was too small which is where most people would have it, so with two caskets and a couch there wasn't much to spare, with kneeling benches out from the caskets and two stands for putting Mass cards, and even that wasn't enough, they started putting them on the caskets till somebody got a box. And flowers, some of them came on stands and we had to have a little table, but after a while they just put them in the bedrooms on the beds, we couldn't put any in Grandfather's bedroom, he had a bad enough time breathing. Every time I went in to check him, that was my main job, he was weeping and writing in a scribbler, especially when there was music, he'd write down requests, mostly in Gaelic, I couldn't read them but the fiddlers would take one look and away they'd go. Mostly sad tunes.

The caskets were pretty big of beautiful wood and golden handles and inside Charlie Dave and Dada were laid out on thick satin like a white quilt. They looked like nothing had happened to them at all, that they just laid down in luxury for a while. I was glad it was me that washed their faces. And that it wasn't their faces that was broken and smashed. They put a big crucifix on the wall over both caskets. Each Christ looked down at his casket with those thorns sticking in his head and blood running down his face, and a slash in his ribs with blood running down from that under the towel they put around him and down his leg, and nails in his hands and feet, he looked a lot worse off than Charlie Dave or Dada. I don't know what we would of had if we'd a had to pay for it ourselves.

Out in the yard they had to go to people's houses and borrow tables to put the food and drink on, and they had to get chairs for old people, and cripples, or people that got sick and couldn't stand up, and of course some people got drunk and couldn't stand up, couldn't even sit up, for that matter, some a them. Like I said, a lot of people treated it like a picnic, especially after they had a few, more than like a funeral. A few of them even started playing horseshoes, the priest had to go over and talk to them.

That's another thing, they had two sisters there all the time, every hour a new two came and said the rosary, they knelt on the floor, so not to take up the space on the kneeling benches which was for the people coming all the time. Each two would go through the whole thing, the glorious mysteries, the sorrowful mysteries, the joyful mysteries, and then they'd talk to us and console us, how sorry they were, how terrible for us, but how lucky we were to have those men at least for a time, short as it was. My mother kind of sniffed behind their backs but I thought they were nice. Not like in school where I was always worried one of them was going to say something to me.

You couldn't believe the amount of people. A lot of relatives I didn't ever know we had. Even Mother didn't know a lot of them, especially on my father's side, though she knew some of them a little from when she got married. They came from Glace Bay and Sydney, and New Waterford, and Dominion, and Port Morien and the Gardiner, everywhere around, and, my mother said, she didn't think one of the men went to the toilet before he came, they had to use the outhouses of all our neighbours, they said they didn't mind, but those that didn't have them sitting over old bootleg pits were worried they were going to get over-full. The honey man must of had quite the week of work after that wake.

It was the people from the country that surprised me. I didn't even know there was the country until then. Oh, I guess I heard talk of relatives I never knew but I always thought they must of been the ones went to Boston, they're the only ones I ever saw, when they came on vacation in the summer, they never stayed with us but I'd meet them at the ball field or hanging around Main Street, or at the house of one of my cousins up in the rows.

The first ones from the country came in an old car, four of them, brothers and sisters, the mother and father couldn't come because they were both sick and couldn't make the trip, they sent a message written in Gaelic to Da, my grandfather, even though they were not my mother's but my father's relatives, they were all from the same place, Mabou, and they talked to him in Gaelic, in the country even the kids could speak Gaelic, and for that matter they even spoke English kinda funny, it was quite the thing to

51

hear them talking to our other cousins from Boston, you'd swear to God everybody was speaking a different language. The Boston crowd were all in suits and dresses we'd never seen the likes of before, and the girls all had their hair done, and the boys had barber haircuts. They had wallets and purses with money in them. The country people had on clothes just like us. They were nice. They talked very quiet, but smart. When one of the Boston crowd asked a smart-aleck question like, "How old is that ka, anyways?" one of them would answer, "Oh well, she's old enough, now, isn't she, Mairi," and Mairi would say, "She is," saying it like she was hissing like a tiny snake, all their English talk had this Gaelic on it, and another one would say, "The old fella himself bought her when he was away, she comes in handy," and they'd never answer the question, because they knew the ones from Boston were just showing off, trying to call attention to their own car, which they came down in and they polished every day. And then the country ones would talk to each other in Gaelic and laugh, which really put up the noses of the ones from Boston. They didn't come for the funeral, they were just already down when the accident happened. Their parents worked in factories, they said, making shoes. They all had good shoes, with buckles on them.

After they met everybody, they said to Mother their parents told them to ask if she wanted them to play some music, and Mother said to ask Father MacDonald, and they talked quite a while with him, he could speak Gaelic too, and they played and sang some tunes. They were really beautiful, especially the songs, even though I couldn't understand a word.

I thought the MacGregor funeral would be bigger than ours but it wasn't. I guess two people in a family, father and son, getting killed in the same accident made ours seem more like a soap opera and more people were interested. Mostly more women. And more from away. All the miners would go. And of course the funeral later was smaller because there was fewer miner's families that were Protestants, and a lot of the women wouldn't go to the Protestant church for fear the priest would frown at them even though the priests never said anything about funerals. But of course all the men, most anyway, went to both of the wakes and funerals.

The MacGregor wake was more like a wake to me.

Like I said, ours turned half into a picnic because there were so many around all the time, and our country cousins playing music, even though it was laments and other sad stuff, it still sort of spruced things up, and people talking and laughing out in the yard, and of course they had their pints in their breast pockets, and it was so odd, kinda comical really, to see all those men in their black suits and black shoes and white shirts and neck ties, it just didn't seem like a wake to me, even though it was my own father and brother in the caskets. It was a good thing in a way because nothing really hit me till after everything was over. Then I felt so bad I couldn't get out of the rocking chair. I didn't think I'd ever get out of it. I didn't want to.

The MacGregor casket was closed. That made it different too. All's you could see was the casket, covered, so it was like it was a box, like there was nobody in it, you really got the feeling of dead, if my father and brother were like that, just two boxes in the room I think I would have bawled through the whole thing instead of after they were in the ground. They had quite a good-sized living room plus a front room and the coffin was in the living room and they had chairs all around the walls and somebody in every chair when I went in and I didn't know what to do. I couldn't sit down and Mother told me they wouldn't have a kneeling bench, they didn't kneel down to pray, "Protestants are a lot like heathens in some ways," she said, I nearly turned and ran, but instead I just walked right up to the coffin and knelt on the floor, and blessed myself and said a few our fathers and hail marys and glory be to the fathers, but I just sort of whipped through them. I felt so stupid praying to a box with nothing in it. I thought, I was so dumb, I found out later they put his bones and stuff in it, whatever was left of him, I was glad I didn't know about it when I thought about it afterwards. I was only on my knees probably a minute but it seemed like forever, I got kind of buzzy in the head, I looked around and saw all the people in black suits, sad, sad faces, everybody with black shoes on and the women with black hats and black veils over their faces, I thought I was going to cry, but I started to giggle, so I streaked for outside but I went the wrong way and instead of the kitchen I landed at the end of the hall next to the front room but I couldn't open the front door to the sun porch. I was twisting it and yanking on it when two hands came down on my shoulders.

It was the minister. Mr. MacLeod. I didn't know him but I knew he was the minister because of the suit. But he knew me. "Margaret," he said, "take it easy, it's O.K. Come, sit down a minute." They sat me down in a sofa chair was so big and deep I thought I would disappear before I stopped dropping, and they gave me a saucer and cup with tea in it, it had a bunch of flowers painted on it, and they made me talk. Mrs. MacGregor was there, and her sister, and Minnie and Morag and Mary, everybody in the family's name started with M.

How are you?

Pretty good.

How is your mother?

Pretty good.

Will she get a chance to come up?

I don't know.

I'm going to try to get down, this evening.

A bunch of questions like that. I didn't know them all that good, because they went to the Protestant school, but

Scenes from the Motion Picture

MARGARET'S MUSEUM

STILL PHOTOGRAPHY BY ANTOINE SAITO

**Margaret alone
in the White Rose Café
(Helena Bonham Carter)**

Neil (Clive Russell) and Margaret—he's been thrown out of the café for playing his bagpipes. Margaret's grandfather (Peter Boretski). Margaret and Neil celebrate their love on the sea cliffs of Glace Bay.

Kenneth Welsh as Angus. Below: Peggy (Andrea Morris) is rescued from the cave-in of a bootleg mine.

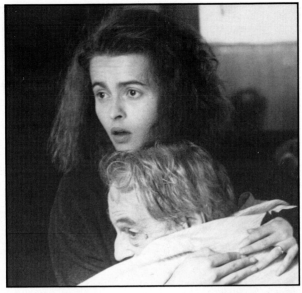

Malofilm Communications presents
a Ranfilm/Imagex/Télé-Action/Skyline Production
Helena Bonham Carter, Kate Nelligan in "Margaret's Museum" with Clive Russell, Craig Olejnik, Andrea Morris, Peter Boretski & Kenneth Welsh as "Angus"— based on a short story by Sheldon Currie; written by Gerald Wexler & Mort Ransen; producers Mort Ransen, Christopher Zimmer, Claudio Luca, Steve Clark-Hall; directed by Mort Ransen; produced with the participation of Telefilm Canada, British Screen Finance, The National Film Board of Canada, Nova Scotia Film Development Corporation, SOGIC. Still photography by Antoine Saito.

Burning of the company store.

Right: Preparing for the wedding. Bottom: Angus (Kenneth Welsh) with Ian (Craig Olejnik).

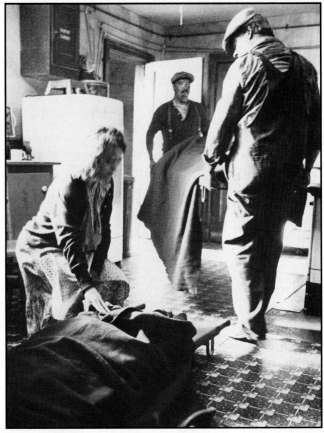

After the mine accident, Margaret has the bodies taken home. Below: Margaret carries the suitcase with the beginnings of her museum.

they were around my age, and my mother sometimes did housework for the MacGregors and when I was younger she'd drag me along 'cause she couldn't leave me home, and I'd play cards with the girls, and when I was older I kept going, sometimes by myself, and they wanted me to come because it's a lot better playing cards with four than with three, and their mother wouldn't play cards, she'd always say, I could have six buns of bread set by the time I'd finish losing a game of auction forty-five.

Maybe it was the tea, but after a while I got more comfortable and Mrs. MacGregor was nice and talked a lot herself, told me she knew how I felt losing a father and brother, and what good men they were, and she said how I'd be thinking I'd never get over it, and that was right, you never do get over it, and that was a good thing, because as long as you don't get over it you'll always have them with you even though they're gone, you can even talk to them, and you can't hear them talk back, but you know what they'd be saying, and especially you can talk to them when you're trying to decide whether to do something or not, because you can be sure the dead will always give good advice.

She said a dead person in the family was like a load you carried on your back, you get used to it, but it's always there, like a mountain climber with a back pack, you even forget about it sometimes, but you always know it's there, it's a weight, but still you're glad it's there, you wouldn't want to be without it because keeping going up the mountain wouldn't make any sense without it. She knew this because her father was killed in the pit. Now she and me were the same, we both had two dead people to carry, and we wish they were still alive, but since they're not we're glad to be the ones to carry them. I was glad my mother wasn't there, she'd of thought Mrs. MacGregor was just showing off, talking like that, she always thought people were showing off if they could do things she couldn't do.

The funeral is where I finally broke down. The two coffins up at the end of the middle aisle in front to the altar rail, they were so beautiful in the house, now they were closed and they reminded me of two big fat brown worms, with the tears in my eyes they even looked like they were moving, and it was all I could do to keep from bawling out crying, though it was the singing and not the coffins that started me off.

They had the men's choir there, they always had it for high mass, especially for a funeral. Sometimes I'd go to mass when there was a funeral just to hear the singing, some people got to think I was holy because I went to mass on a week day, but it was for the singing. I loved that tune it starts out *Dies irae dies illa,* I used to have more lines of it memorized, it was in the prayer book in Latin and translated in English, but the English didn't seem like much, isn't it funny how in a strange language a person can't understand something means more in a song. Anyway, when they started the *Dies Irae* the tears started to roll like marbles down my face.

Now it makes me laugh. I don't know why, but it makes me laugh to think of me standing there, it was all so awful and so beautiful, listening to that lovely song and thinking of my father and my brother like two caterpillars inside two big worms, and when the song stopped the priest read the gospel, I'll never forget the first line of it was Martha talking to Jesus and said, If you had of been here, my brother wouldn't of died. I thought she was giving him a piece of her mind, and I was right with her, but then she seemed to change her mind, and then they had this talk I didn't understand much of it, but it was supposed to make you feel better, but I didn't feel any better, and I stopped crying, and I started to get like I thought Martha was at the start of the gospel, I started to think, the thought just kept going through my mind, I don't want to put up with this, I just don't want to put up with it.

Chapter Four

The Beach and the Card Game

MAYBE IT MAKES ME laugh now because when I think about it, meeting Neil later, that's the way he was, he didn't want to put up with stuff. Maybe that's why I loved him so much. Like the time the very evening we met, and the two Chinamen flung him out of the White Rose Café. I'm sure it was true that if he wasn't too drunk he would have got me to mind his bagpipes, and he would have gone in and took them on. Even if he knew he'd get the shit kicked out of him.

And then there was another time, God, how could I forget it. At the beach. Neil loved the water. Never to swim in it though. He'd seldom swim. He loved to skip rocks, but mostly he'd just look, stare into the distance, and sometimes he'd shake his head, and sometimes he'd mumble, "those bastards." Once we moved to Glace Bay, our house, this house, as you can see, is right on the ocean. He'd stand out on the cliff, especially on a windy day when the ocean was boiling and spuming and he'd play his pipes, and mutter in Gaelic, and he'd come in the house and he'd be cross, but not at me, and he'd be laughing too, and I'd say what are you laughing at you idiot and he'd say something, I wouldn't know why he was saying it, I understand him better now, like he'd say, "You know, Mairead"—when he'd say my name he'd always say it in Gaelic—"Mairead," he'd say, "if it wasn't for that bit of water out there you could walk right up on the shore of the Isle of Skye," and then he'd sing the "Isle of Skye" in Gaelic, and then for me he'd sing it in English something like, "Here is the man, born to be king, over the sea from Skye," I can't really remember it, and he'd tell me the story behind the song, he knew all that stuff, which is why him and my grandfather got along so well, I guess. My grandfather had a lot of that stuff written down in his scribblers, it's still there for anybody to read, Neil used to go over them and over them once he found out what was in them, but I didn't like him to because everytime he did, he'd end up shaking his head back and forth and back and forth and going "Jesus, Jesus, Jesus," and getting crosser and crosser, till he almost scared me, though he never spoke a cross word to me; but then he'd get out the pipes and wail away for an hour, and then he'd be okay, and he'd smile at me, and he'd say, one thing you can say for all that misery, the music that came out of it was awful good stuff. If Ian was around he'd always say something sarcastic when Neil talked like that, but it never bothered Neil, he'd say, "You know, John," he'd call him by his name in English, John instead of Ian, 'cause that always got Ian's goat, "You know, John," he'd say, "it's a lot like moonshine, you take oats or barley, boil it in molasses till it screams, and out of all that misery comes this awful good stuff; you can't sing it, but it sure makes you want to sing." Of course Ian never sang a note in his life, even drunk. But talk politics, that was a whole other thing. It used to make me mad. The two of them sitting at the table, one at each end with a glass, and the bottle on the table between them, and Ian at one end giving a speech, you'd think he was at the pit head haranguing a bunch of miners, and Neil at the other end singing you'd think he was down at the Assumption Hall giving a concert, both at the same time, neither one of them listening to the other one, and me wanting to go for a walk down to the wharf and look at the fishing boats, or watch the kids jumping off the wharf and swimming in the harbour, and the seagulls flying around like little screeching airplanes. I loved doing that because when we did it Neil always did this great talking, my God, when I think of it, he was a great talker, and I always thought of him as a singer and piper, and Ian as the talker. Of course, I could always understand Ian. He wasn't any smarter than me for all his talk. I was glad Neil talked so much, because he never noticed that I never had much to say, naturally, because I didn't know anything, except what I learned in school, and all I could remember of that was that the square on the long side of a right-angled triangle is equal to the sum of the squares on the other two sides, and believe it or not, the situation doesn't come up too often where it seems the right thing to blurt that out. Although I did do it once. With Neil of course, you could say anything to him, and he'd make something out of it.

We were playing cards, steal the pack, with Ian and his girl friend, he had a girl friend then, girl friend! It was the mine manager's daughter, Peggy, and of course a Protestant, I didn't think she was serious, I thought she was going with Ian to get her father's goat. Ian, of course thought she was crazy about him, but I knew she never took him to her place, and that was a sign, but Ian never paid any attention to signs. He was showing off while we played cards by shooting off his mouth about unions. The miner will never get anywhere until he gets organized. You can't expect management to just hand over money and benefits to the miner. We have to be as strong as they are and then they'll have to negotiate, and the only way to be strong without money is to be organized. Now, Neil, is that right or is that wrong?

And Neil said, "They'll send in the army."

"Who?"

"The government. If the miner gets strong, he'll have to go on strike. Then there's no coal. So for the government, that's an emergency. They'll send in the army. That's what they always do. You have to be pretty strong to be stronger than the army," Neil said.

"How do you know that's what they always do, you've only been here two years."

"We've been here for a long, long time, John," Neil said, using his English name. "You just don't remember. Do you remember 1745, John?"

"I guess nobody remembers 1745, eh." Even Ian knew he already lost the argument. You couldn't argue with Neil because he knew too much and he knew how to get you. He'd play with Ian for a while like he was a fish and then he'd yank him up on the wharf like a little herring.

"Go and read your grandfather's scribblers, John," Neil said. "He remembers. His blood was there, spilled on the ground, and our blood was there, spilled on the ground. He remembers, I remember, and if you don't remember, go and put your ear on his chest, and listen to his lungs singing, and maybe it will tickle your memory."

"What do you think?" Neil said to me.

And I said, "I think, that the square on the long side of a right-angle triangle is equal to the sum of the squares on the other two sides."

"I don't think anybody could have put it any better. So

why don't we just play cards now that we know where everybody stands."

"What do you say, Peggy?" Ian said, trying his best to have the last word, even if it didn't mean anything.

"I need to use the washroom," Peggy said.

"O.K.," Ian said. He went to the cupboard and got a flashlight and handed it to her and she couldn't for the life of her figure out why he was giving her a flashlight. I could see her thinking, did I ask him for a flashlight? But finally it dawned on her, and a good thing because nobody quite knew how to tell her, not that she was stupid and didn't know there was such a thing as an outhouse, but they didn't have one at her house, and she never used one, and I suppose even if you imagined yourself using one you'd imagine yourself doing it in the daytime light. She took the flashlight and she went out the door and I don't know if she had her pee or not, but she didn't have time to make it to the outhouse and back. I didn't blame her for being scared, I didn't like going out there alone myself and I was used to it, and she'd be lucky if she didn't get her nice black patent leather shoes wet even though she had the light.

But I was telling you about the beach.

We went to the beach for a walk. We loved to start at one end of the beach, the Dominion side and walk along the breaking waves in our bare feet across to the Lingan side and go across the bridge there and if lobsters was in season we'd buy some and borrow a pot from a fisherman and cook them and eat them right there, and drink beer with them. Oh, God, you talk about good.

So one evening we went to the beach, me and Neil and Ian and Peggy, he was still going with Peggy then although I thought it was wearing pretty thin, but I guess she was starting to like him and was just worried about the trouble she'd have if she decided to marry him, she'd have to become a Catholic, it was always the girl that turned in those days, though not always, you could have a mixed marriage, but like the priest often said when he talked about marriage in church, "the church frowns on mixed marriages."

Anyway, we were walking across the beach in our dresses and sweaters because it was a little cool at the end of the summer and Ian and Neil were walking and talking together and Peggy and me were behind, and I wanted to listen to the men because they were at it again and I always enjoyed that because Neil always got the best of it, and anyway it was usually about something interesting that I didn't know anything about, but I couldn't listen to them because Peggy kept going on and on about her brother spilling ink on her good sweater which was why she had to wear the one she had on, which was a lot better than the one I had on, she wasn't mean, she just didn't notice, I thought she'd never stop, and I couldn't believe anybody could think of so much to say about it more than "he spilt ink on my sweater, I had to wear this one," but she kept on and on, she could of written a book on it, so I decided to just ask her, probably just to shut her up. So I put my hand on her arm at the elbow and slowed us down so the boys would be ahead more, and I stared at her till she turned, and looked at me.

"What?" she said.

"Are you thinking about getting married to Ian?"

Well I guess she thought that was quite a change of the topic of the conversation. She stopped stalk still. She got beet red in the face. She looked at me like I maybe pulled off her sweater and left her standing there in her bra. Her mouth hung open I could see the bottoms of all her top teeth. Her arms hung down like she was holding two coal scuttles. Then she tried to talk. I felt so sorry for her but even so I could hardly keep from laughing, I was even a little scared, though I knew she couldn't beat me, never mind how long she was I'd a flattened her, I suppose she could of kicked me one in the shin before I could do a thing about it, but she couldn't even talk let alone kick. She started sputtering stuff, "You.......What..........Him.....," like she was starting to say things she didn't want to say or didn't dare say, she went on for quite a while like that and then she started to sob and I put my arms around her and hugged her so she couldn't see me laughing, and she put her arms around me and there we stood in each other's arms on the evening beach, like Miss Mutt and Miss Jeff, and me laughing and her sobbing away, and she talked then through my hair, she said "He'll never ask me" and "I wouldn't be allowed." And Ian's voice boomed down the beach, something, I don't know what, and we looked and saw they had got way ahead of us, and were standing looking at us, and we started walking and she said, "Go slow, I don't want to catch up till they can't tell I was crying." The tide was coming in and the little waves were splatting at our feet, so we took off our shoes and put our nylons in them and walked in the water, the foam running all around our ankles and I held her shoes while she made a cup with her hands and rinsed off her face. Then I did it too, for the tears running down my face from laughing.

I wasn't just laughing at her. I was laughing because I was happy. She was the daughter of the big shot and she was crying because she couldn't have my brother. At long last it wasn't me who was the laughing stock. Here I was doing one of the nicest things in the world you can do. I was up to my ankles in the Atlantic Ocean, my shoes in my hand, my nylons in my shoes, walking slow across Dominion beach, slowly catching up to Ian and thinking, this is great, this is going to take forever, it's too bad she got something to cry about and can't enjoy herself. Yes, it was a far cry from the way my life used to be.

I don't really know why they made fun of me or wouldn't talk to me in the dressing room, or walk with me. Sometimes they would but mostly they wouldn't. They made fun of me for my runny nose but I don't know if that was it. There was always a few kids got picked on and I was just one of them.

Maybe I was a tomboy. When it came to playing games it was a different story. Like for games I was always one of the first ones picked. One of our big games we played was peggy because you could play it when it was too late for hockey because the ice was rotten and it was too muddy and slushy to get on the ball field. I liked peggy because it was the nickname for Margaret, though nobody ever called me Peggy and I always wished they would. I even said, "Just call me Peggy," but they never did. But once Neil called me by my Gaelic name then I didn't want anything but that. Peggy was a great game because you didn't have to wait on somebody passing you the puck like in hockey, or they'd stick you out in right field in baseball if you were a girl and they had to let you play because they didn't have enough. Like in marbles, if you were good at it they couldn't stop you without cheating.

In Peggy you took a picket from a picket fence and that was the bat, and you made as big a circle on the ground as you could by standing in the middle and stretching. The peggy was a piece of broom handle about five inches long sharpened at both ends and that was like the ball. The pitcher threw the peggy at the circle with you standing in it and if it landed in the circle you were out. If you hit the peggy and someone caught it you were out. But if nobody caught it you went to it and hit it on one of the sharp ends and when it flew in the air you tried to hit it again. You had three chances to do that. Then one of the players tried to throw the peggy from where it was into the circle. If it went in the circle you were out. And if three people got out the team was out. But if he missed the circle then you paced off the difference between the circle and the peggy and if you paced off five, that was your score. I was good at peggy. Even after they wouldn't let me play baseball or hockey because I was a girl, they still picked me almost first for peggy. But after the game they pretended I wasn't around.

But after I met Neil I never wanted to play games anyway. That stuff was all behind me. Then I loved walking across the beach, because it was so long and so beautiful there, either day or night, but especially at night if it was warm and the moon was out, and sometimes the moon was low and spread the light all over the water. And even when you got over to the Lingan side and talked to the fishermen and maybe cooked and ate some lobsters and drank some beer, you had the whole beach to walk back talking, or singing, and kicking the water. When I think of it, God, there I was with a house of my own, and a husband that worked and only drank on the weekends or holidays and even then he wasn't too bad if Ian wasn't around; I enjoyed even sitting down alone, or doing the dishes, or washing Neil's clothes, or just cleaning the house. I might have got tired of it but I didn't think I would.

All I ever thought I'd like to have more was a baby to feed and change and talk to and sing to, especially sing to now I had all those songs Neil taught me. I never did get a baby. If I had got pregnant, when everything else was gone, I still would have had a boy or a girl to talk to and sing to all my life. Even just to have someone to tell all that happened would have been quite the thing. Someone to walk across the beach with and talk to and sing to. Every year a little older and wanting to hear the story again because it would be a little different each year, never quite the same, changing as we got older.

That evening we all were walking across was one of those quiet evenings, not a breath of air, me and Peggy, she had the same nickname I'd wanted, were still way behind the men, holding our shoes and nylons in one hand and our skirts up from the water and kicking the water with our toes, when we heard them yelling at us, we couldn't hear what they were saying but they were beckoning to hurry up, so we got out of the water and ran up the beach.

"Are you two going steady, or what?" Ian said to Peggy.

"There's something happening up ahead," Neil said.

We could hear people yelling, but we couldn't see anything until we got around the sand dune near where the channel goes through at Lingan. A big whale was half up on the shore. A whole lot of people were thrashing around. Someone put a ladder up and there were kids and even older people on top of it and dancing, and falling off into the water or the sand. Somebody punched a hole in it and was filling a bottle full of blood. I couldn't believe my eyes. We stood there for a while, it seemed like a long time, in front of the sand dune, watching. Peggy was saying, over and over again, "My God, my God, my God." There were two fishing boats behind it, looked like the men on it were trying to figure out how to do something, later I realized they were trying to tie a rope around it to try to pull it out into the water. Later they told us the whale had got in the channel and tried to turn around and got stuck on the shore just as the tide was going out so quick that soon there was not enough water under it so it could work its way back into the water.

Neil said something and started to walk toward the whale. I couldn't make out what he said, but Ian said, "Never mind, Neil, leave it alone." But Neil never stopped. He went down and stood in front of a man who was standing in front of the whale's face and spitting in its eye. I started after Neil but Ian grabbed my hand and kept me back. "Wait," he said. So we couldn't hear what they were saying down there, but we could see. Neil said something, and the man said something and Neil said something, and the man spit in the whale's eye. Then Neil spit in the man's eye. Then the man walloped Neil in the mouth and he went to the ground, and Ian let me go. By the time I got there Neil was up on his feet and swinging, and Ian was swinging, and all the man's friends were swinging and all I could do was stand in the sand and watch. Me and Peggy and the whale watching all hell break loose.

Ian was tough but he wasn't Charlie Dave. Even Charlie Dave I don't think could of beat his way through that bunch. They beat the pulp out of the two of them. Then the mounties came. There was a lot of talking and milling around. I don't know if Ian and Neil were out cold or just too sore to move. They just laid there in the sand. The fishermen came and put them in their lobster boat and we got in and they took us over to the wharf side. They put the two men in a fisherman's shack that had two bunks in it. They gave them a drink of rum and we wiped the blood off them, They were O.K. but sore. After about fifteen minutes they sat up on the bunks with their feet on the floor and without a word Ian bought a quart of rum from a fisherman. After about ten more minutes of silence and rum Ian said, "You goddamn idiot. Didn't I tell you to stay put."

"Well, Jesus, John, didn't you see what was going on?"

"I'm not blind. I saw what was going on. It wasn't our business."

"How would you like somebody spittin in your face?"

"For Christ sake, Neil, it's only a goddamn whale."

"And you're only a goddamn coal miner—do you like what they're doing to you?"

"Like what?"

"Look at the goddamn whale, *John*. Just look at it. Stand still, or sit still, in your case, and look at it. It was just trying to live its life. When it needed a little help, some arsehole came along and spit in its eye. Look at the whale, *John*, and read your grandfather's notebooks."

They kept it up, and kept it up. They argued all the way back across the beach, spoiling the moon. When I got home I tried to write down everything they said, but all I could remember was Neil saying to Ian that he agreed that a union would be a help but the best thing would be if they didn't work in a pit at all. And Ian said, sure, let's start a farm in the back yard, we got at least fifty square feet, we'll grow all our own vegetables, and keep a cow and a pig and a couple of beef cattle, and some chickens and turkeys, and for money to buy beer and pay the light bill we'll rent you and your pipes out to concerts. That's all I could remember. It's the first time Ian ever got the best of Neil. I guess that's why I remembered that. Later, after they were all dead, I still remembered so I wrote it down in Grandfather's scribbler where he left off just before he died. I saw my name on the page in the last sentence that he wrote, and I was so excited I could feel the hair on my neck, but I didn't read the page then, I went back to the beginning. That's when I realized my grandfather wasn't the one who started the scribblers. A whole bunch of them from the beginning were written down by Dada's mother who was Morag who was one of the first women to come to Reserve Mines from the country. She started out.... Well, look, I'll show you the start, you can read the rest when you like:

"This wunt be written great for I am writen it in english for fear none will be able to read it in the gallick for I can see how things are going." I started there and I read all through hers and all through Grandfather's who she left them with to keep going when she died, I went right through till I came back again to my name in the last sentence he wrote: "It's kinda comical if it wasn't so sad, after the english army killed the half of us and then our own politicians gave us the boot we came here and started up and before you know we gave our own land away to work in a hole in the ground, gave ourselves the boot, like Morag always said, I learned it from her but I learned it too late and now there's Margaret married to the only one you'd think wouldn't work in the pit but there he is working in it anyway, and him working with Ian, if the two of them get killed what will the poor girl do." That was his last sentence. It was like he almost knew, like he predicted what would happen; all my men that I had left, died in the one day, and he could feel it coming when he wrote that down. And then he wrote down a poem in it, which Morag used to do, though she used to put the poems down more often than not in Gaelic with the English after it, I don't know if she copied them out of a book or made them up herself, but his was after one of hers, he changed some of the words or he changed the second line I guess, here it is here. "Seventeen hundred and forty-five, hardly half of them left alive; nineteen hundred and forty-four, half in the pit, half in the war."

That's when I started to write in the scribblers. I still didn't know what happened in 1745 and I was always a bit like Ian, who cares? but now I decided I would look it up. The first words I wrote in the scribbler, right after Grandfather's little poem was "wonder of wonders, miracle of miracles, Neil agreed that Ian was right about something." He much as admitted that Ian was right about the unions, and for the first time between the two of them Ian got the last real word. After that I began to think about Ian more.

Chapter Five
The Circus and the Union

IT WAS CHARLIE DAVE I loved and still do, but I think about Ian a lot now. I liked him then and he was good to me too, but it was Charlie Dave that I loved. It's not just that Ian got killed too, and with Neil at that, that my like turned to love, although you do think a lot more about people when they're dead. The thing is I've come to see there was more to Ian than I thought. They were so different, Charlie Dave and Ian, you'd never take them for brothers. They looked alike, I don't mean that. They were different in their heads and their hearts. Like fighting, for instance. Charlie Dave was great. I was kicked around like a yappy dog as it was, I'd hate to think what would of happened if he wouldn't have been around. But I remember now how it felt like when I went to him and told him somebody did something to me, hit me or stole my kerchief, or my mitts. He was almost glad. Now, I think he was glad and he'd either go right away if it was something stolen and get it back, he always got it back or he'd get something the same or just as good or better, or he'd wait till he'd meet the person that did it and he'd beat the living shit right out of him. What I mean is, he loved it. He was as quiet a person as you could imagine, and he'd never pick a fight in a million years any more than he would hurt somebody or even an animal for nothing. But give him a reason and he just loved to fight. I think that's why he was so good at it. He just loved it.

Ian was altogether different. I don't think Ian liked to fight. I think he hated it. When he was doing it he looked like he was scared he was going to hurt the guy. He beat him just as bad as Charlie Dave, but it was altogether different.

So since he died my mind keeps going back to Ian and I realize now that there he was between Charlie Dave who all his friends and family liked so much and everybody else was scared of and Neil who could play the pipes and sing and knew all kinds of history and stuff so nobody could argue with him and nobody was thinking about what Ian was good at and what he was good at was probably what everybody needed most at the time.

I think the first inkling I got was from Peggy, his girl. I began to think a lot better of her as time went along. She was spoiled but why shouldn't she be spoiled she had everything handed to her, but here she was going against her family for Ian, that must have been awful hard; she was good looking and of course had nice clothes, and no problems like me with a runny nose and quite a few of the boys in the Protestant school were after her, so why should she go out with Ian and make everybody cross at her, even her friends, although they really envied her, doing things they'd never dare do, pretended to be against her and of course they burned with gossip behind her back; but she put up with it all just to go out with Ian. She said to me once, it must be nice to have a brother so gentle; it really startled me, her saying that, all I could think was, who? is she talking about my brother Ian? That's when I began to think about Ian in a different way and I remembered how nice he was to animals, even ones other people hated, I saw him kissing a mouse once, and carrying it around the house petting it, he even tamed it; my mother had a conniption fit one day when she walked in on him asleep on his back and the mouse asleep on his forehead. Other people had dogs and cats, but Ian would have salamanders and turtles, he'd go out and find them God knows where, nobody in Reserve Mines ever saw things like that unless Ian had them, and if he didn't have something queer like that, he'd have something normal, but not anything like anybody else would have or even want to have, like a snake or a bug.

One time a circus came to town and one of the shows they had was snakes and this guy outside the tent had a boa constrictor wrapped around his neck and when he had a crowd he offered ten dollars to anybody who would take it off of him, and in two seconds Ian was right up there. The guy said, never mind sonny, you're too little, and before the guy could blink Ian grabbed it off him, and the guy grabbed it back and the two of them pulled it back and forth, back and forth like they were playing tug o' war, the snake was just like a rope, first it was coiled but then it was stretched out with the man on one end and Ian on the other until Charlie Dave pulled the man off and Ian coiled it up like a lasso and pulled it over his head like a hat with a hole in the top of it. Well then it was quite a brouhaha because the man wouldn't give Ian the ten and was accusing him of stealing his snake, and the crowd was yelling give him his money he did what you said, and Charlie Dave put his finger under the man's chin and said give him the ten, and then another circus man came over with a cop, but it wasn't a mountie it was only Angus MacEachern, the town cop we called him, even though Reserve Mines wasn't a town, and the circus man said I want this man arrested for stealing the snake, and Angus said well what's the story Ian, and Ian explained the situation, all the time stroking the boa constrictor which was now showing some signs of life, and the circus men when they noticed this started to look worried and said things like, this is a dangerous animal if it gets hungry, this is a dangerous animal we had it doped up but the stuff is wearing off, but Ian was stroking it with not a care in the world, and Charlie Dave with his finger under the circus man's chin, every time he moved the finger went with him, and every time he moved Charlie Dave said, give him the ten, and Angus started getting nervous of the snake too, and he knew even if the snake was out of the way he'd still have to deal with Charlie Dave, nobody would put it past him to hit a cop if you gave him a good reason. Of course the crowd around now was enormous, and Ian uncoiled the snake from around his neck and had it wrapped around his arm and the snake was really starting to squirm, and he said to the circus man, O.K., I'm going to give you back your snake now, and the guy jumped back behind the table was in front of the tent, and Ian went around after him and then they were going round and round the table, and the crowd was laughing, and the guy was yelling take it inside and put it in the cage, and Ian said, give me the money first. So he threw the ten dollars on the table and Ian went in the tent. Of course the man made a fortune that night. He put his price up from ten cents to fifteen cents to get in the tent and he had by then almost everybody in Reserve Mines standing there with money in their pockets, and they already got their money's worth in entertainment, Ian was more of a circus than the circus. Yes, he was always good with animals, I always knew that, but I didn't know he was good with people because his chance never came up until the strike.

Yes. He was the one who knew what was good for the miners. And he was the one who got them organized. He surprised me and he surprised himself. When he got the men to go out on strike he could hardly believe it. I think what happened, what got him going, was when Neil agreed with him, said he was right after all about how the miners needed a decent union; it made him more sure of himself. For all he argued against Neil, he admired him and thought he was smart, so when Neil gave in it made Ian sure he was right and you could see after that when he talked to the men they were with him.

I think that's what Peggy saw in him. He would do things he didn't want to do, he just made himself do them and that made her brave too to face her father and mother. They didn't even bother to warn her not to go out with him because of religion, everybody knew that was the thing anyway, on both sides, they just told her he was a troublemaker, which of course he was, he certainly made trouble for the company, he got all the men out. It wasn't the president of the union that did it, it was Ian. Neil was amazed with what he was doing. I was too.

Anyhow, that Saturday night Peggy and Ian and Neil and me played cards and it was nothing but union talk, strike talk. How could people survive. Ian was beginning to think it would work. Neil was not so sure. "If things get tough," he said, "will the men stay out? Will the women let them?"

Well, Ian twigged to that right away. "That's right," he said. "The men might stay out if the women wouldn't push them back. We need the women to back up the men. We need somebody to talk to the women, to explain how much we'll be better off if we all stick together." He looked at me when he said that.

"You think I'm gonna talk to every coal miner's wife in Reserve?" I said.

"It's not just Reserve," he said. "It's every colliery. We'd have to get people in every colliery to call meetings of groups of women and explain the situation. If the women back the men up we could do it. We'd all be better off." He looked at me again.

"I'd do it," I said, "but I don't know how."

"I'll do it too," Peggy said. Maybe she surprised herself. And like death or a movie she no sooner said it when the big knock came on the door. Peggy's father.

In he comes when Neil opens the door in a nice top-coat. He stood with his hands in his topcoat pockets. I thought if he came he'd come roaring, but no, you could tell he didn't like doing it, he had to. He waited quite a while before he spoke.

"Peggy. Your mother wants you to come home."

"Why? What's the matter?"

"Nothing's the matter. She just wants you to come home. She sent me down to get you."

"Well, if nothing's the matter, why do I have to go home?"

"Your mother wants you to come home."

"It's only eight o'clock. Do I have to be in this early, for God's sake? It's only eight o'clock."

"Just for tonight. Your mother wants you home."

"I don't want to go home. I'm having fun here. I'm playing cards. What's wrong with that?"

"Nothing," he said. He couldn't think of anything to say. He just kept on looking and saying it over and over,

"Your mother wants you home." We couldn't say anything, of course. It was between them. We just sat there like dummies with cards in our hands. And he stood there. I nearly laughed out loud.

Finally, she folded up her cards and put them on the table, and walked down the hall to where her coat hung. "I have to get my coat," she said on the way. We could hear the rustle of her getting on her coat, we couldn't see down the hall, and then we heard the back door slam. She went out the back door.

He stood there for a minute. "Where'd she go?" he said.

"Out the back door," Ian said.

He ran after her through the back door, but he was back in five minutes. He stood there looking at us. Just stood there. You couldn't tell if he was cross, or mixed up, or just waiting for someone to speak.

"Maybe she went home," Ian said.

He looked at Ian. "Are you Ian?"

"That's me."

"I have to warn you, Ian, to stay away from my girl."

"Or what?" Ian said, smiling.

"Or you might lose your job."

"Is that right."

"Yes. That is right."

"Well," Ian said, "once we're married, if I don't have a job, who's going to pay the bills? You. Maybe."

He looked like he really wanted to slap Ian's face, but of course he didn't dare. Ian didn't look like he'd take a slap in the face.

"My daughter won't marry the likes of you, young man. I can guarantee you that."

"Wouldn't that be up to her?" Ian said. "And maybe me. What have you got to do with it?"

"She's my daughter."

"And is she going to marry who you tell her to?"

"Well, she's not going to marry you."

"That's what you think."

"That's what I know."

"No," Ian said. "That's what you think. Why don't you ask her? If you can find her."

"I don't want you to take her here any more."

"I didn't take her here," Ian said. "She came here."

We were all still sitting down with cards in our hands. Then Neil got into it.

"Mr. MacDougall," he said, "why don't you go home and see if Peggy is there."

"Who are you?"

"Well. One thing I am is the owner of the floor you're standing on. You are welcome to stand on it, but I think you and us've got done everything we're going to get done here tonight. Your daughter is not here. And I don't think you're gonna like the talk."

He stood there with his hands in the pockets of his nice topcoat. Considering, I guess, or maybe he just didn't know what to do. Him with his hands in his pockets and us with the cards in our hands would of made quite a picture on a calendar. Then he kind of shook his head and out the door. I thought he'd slam it but he didn't. I would've.

He wasn't long gone when she came back, hung up her coat again down the hall, went to the kitchen and washed her hands at the sink, and sat down and picked up her hand of cards and bid 30 for 60 and we all burst out laughing.

"I'm on a losing streak," she said, "I might as well lose big."

Her face was all over black she looked like a coal miner in a dress and sweater, and when we stopped laughing we kept staring at her, smiling.

"What?" she said. "What? What are ya gawkin at?"

"Would you give us a dollar if we guessed where you hid out on your father?"

"What are ya gettin at?"

"Your face is all black, dear. You must of hid out in the coal house."

"Oh my God, don't tell me. Yes I did. I got it all over my hands, it was so dark in there, I must a put them onto my face, is it very much?"

"Don't worry about it, Peg. It looks cute," Ian said.

"Don't you be laughing at me Ian MacNeil, your own face is hard enough to look at even when it's not black," she said, and she stuck out her tongue at him and squinched her mouth and eyes just to make sure he knew she was joking, and that she knew he was teasing her, because that was a lot for her to say, so you could tell she must have been excited, and of course who could blame her, having a fight with her father.

But I twigged to something else. Not long before that night in the same situation she would have shrieked, and streaked to a mirror, and then to the kitchen sink and washed off her face, and looked in the mirror again and got her coat and took off. Maybe it was the fight with her father that made the change in her right then and there, because she was really saying that she knew it didn't matter to Ian to see her like that, that she didn't mind if he did, which is as much as to say she wouldn't mind if he put his big hand up under the back of her sweater and unbuttoned her dress, and that's when I knew, my God maybe they would get married, which got me excited, I looked at Neil and he just had a silly smile on his face and looked his eyes to the ceiling, and I looked at Ian and his eyes looked like they were looking at the back of the inside of his own head, so I knew he was just sitting there with a smirk, playing stupid cards and getting horny. So who knows? Maybe his hand was already into her dress. That, to this day, I don't know. But other than that, the messages all were there for a good card player to pick up on. We were all good card players.

That's the way we were when her father came back. We were having so much fun we didn't hear the knock, if he knocked; what I think he probably did was look in the window, see she was there and burst right in without the knock. The radio was on and Alonso Marsh was singing "Mairi Von" and he went right over and turned it off as if he owned the place. I remember the words to this day they kept singing themselves over and over in my head all evening in my head, "Oh she was tall and slender, and gentle as a fawn, And a smile she had for everyone, but her kisses were only for me, Oh the night I went with Mairi Von a boating on Loch Lee." And it happened so fast we still sat there like the minute before he came in, me laughing my little laugh, Neil with his sly smile on, Ian with a hard-on, and Peggy with black all over her face.

When he turned from the radio he looked so angry that Neil jumped up from the table for fear he'd have to be ready to take him on. Ian would of jumped up too, but of course he couldn't, he had to sit there with his back to him, his head twisted around. I didn't know how long it took for a hard-on to go to a hard-off, so I really felt sorry for Ian. I just sat there. Peggy just sat there.

"Well, Margaret," he said. He sounded like a foghorn talking to a dog. I looked up at him, but he wasn't talking to me. I was startled because I thought he was, because I forgot her name was Margaret too. I thought of her as a peggy, like the little stick in the game, sharp at both ends. Ian said to me once, "She's a very sharp girl, Peggy is." And I said, "Is she sharp at both ends, Ian?" And he said, "That's for me to know and you to find out." And I said, "I'm only interested in the top end." And he went red as a flag. He never said that to me again, although I heard him say it to other people, but not when he knew I could hear him. He was touchy about things like that.

"Well, Margaret," her father said again. His thumbs were stuck in his topcoat pocket and his fingers were flapping up and down. "Let's go." Her face was away from him and her hands up over it, but I don't think she was covering the coal dust smeared all over it, I think she forgot about it, because she took down her hands and turned to him.

"My God. Margaret. Look at your face," he said. She

just looked at him. I expected her to run down the hall and out the door without even stopping for her coat. I had my eye on that coat. But just like she didn't shriek off before when we laughed at her face, she just sat there and looked at her father. I knew then for sure she was struck on Ian and knew she could count on him. She had full lips but when she looked at her father there was nothing but a line like a crayon mark for a mouth at the bottom of her black face. Little tears like tiny silver ball bearings rolled in little furrows down through the coal dust. It wasn't like she was crying. It was like her eyes were like little dippers full of water dripping out over the little furrows dippers have in them for pouring out the water. Her hands were crossed on her lap.

"I'm not going," she said

"You'll break your mother's heart."

"What about my heart?"

"You have a young heart. Your mother has an old heart. There are thousands of boys in the world. You only have one mother."

I thought that was a pretty good one. That was like the kind of thing Neil could say, right off the top of his head. I

99

thought he had her there. I think it would have got me. But, no sir.

"My mother doesn't even talk to me," she said, the red crayon mark on her face hardly moving like the man I saw at a show with a puppet. If you didn't know she was talking you'd think the words were just popping into the air out of nowhere or from an invisible puppet.

"Your mother loves you. She doesn't know how to talk to you any more. That's understandable. Time will take care of that. She needs you home."

"She doesn't need me. She doesn't want me home. She just doesn't want me here." She was saying the words one at a time like they came in little packages. "Yesterday she told me she was going to send me to Mabou to go to school."

"She wants you to get a good education."

"I know what Mabou is."

"Mabou is a very good school."

"Yes. It's a very good school for troubled girls. I found out all about it. I know a girl who went there."

"It's a regular school there. You'd only be going for one year, to finish off."

"There's the regular school and there's the boarding school, which is where they send troubled girls, whatever they are. And it's a Catholic school, for the love a God, I thought she wanted to get me away from the Catholics."

"You know she wants what's best for you."

"I know exactly what she wants. She wants what she wants. She wants to get me away from my friends because they're not her friends. She's frightened I'll get pregnant and have to marry a Catholic." She opened her mouth after she said that as if she couldn't believe her own ears what her mouth just said. "She wants me to go out with What's-his-name, who when I did go out with him he took me to the library to do homework. She wants me to leave my friends who I have fun with and go to the library with What's-his-name. What the hell's his name?" Nothing. And Peggy kept talking anyhow: "And then she wants me to go away altogether for a year to go to a school it's like some kind of prison even worse than the one I'm in at least now I get out overnight. She does not want what I want." She put every word out like she was putting down a card on the table.

"What do you want, Margaret?"

"I just want a little bit of fun too," she said, and she blew a few little tears off of her lips, "I'm doing all right in school. I don't need a little army of nuns to teach me that the square on the hypotenuse of a right-angled triangle is equal to the sum of the square on the other two sides. I know all about squares and I don't like them. I like my friends better." She smiled. This was a new side of her that was coming out for a while now, making jokes. It was quite a thing to see her laughing and crying at the same time. The father didn't know what to do. He knew by now that he couldn't just say something like, "Come, Margaret, that's enough, I'm taking you home now." He knew she wouldn't go. He knew he couldn't make her. She knew it, and he knew she knew it.

"So you just want to have a little fun."

"Yes."

"And is that what you're having now, a little fun?"

"Yes."

"Playing cards, is that what you call fun?"

"Yes. I love playing cards. And I love music. He plays music. And he sings, and we play hockey, and we play ball, and we play peggy, and we play cricket, and we go for walks on the beach, and we have little parties with the fishermen and eat lobsters and drink beer, and we tell jokes, and we're laughing half the time. Before I came here I hardly ever laughed at all."

"Well, there's nothing here to laugh about as far as I'm concerned."

"Well, that's probably true, because what we're doing here tonight is planning a strike for the coal miners to get a decent wage, and I don't suppose you'd find that anything to laugh about."

He couldn't believe his ears. He could not believe his ears. His face looked like somebody stabbed him in the belly and he couldn't even bend over or grab at it to stop the pain. "You are going to help the miners against your own father." He was talking like her now, saying the words one at a time.

"It's not against you. It's against the company. You're not the company. You work for them just like Ian does."

"I don't work for them just like Ian does. I'm the manager. What are they going to say when they see my daughter going around organizing a strike?"

"Well, you used to be a miner. And someday Ian might be the manager. What's the difference? Anyway, I'm not organizing the strike. Ian is. I'm just helping out."

"And just exactly what are you doing to help out?"

"Never mind that," Neil said. "We'll let you know our plans when the time is right."

"I'll guarantee you this, Mr. Man. Whether I know your plans or not, no matter who helps out, even suppose I helped you out myself, your plans won't work. You can go on strike, but you won't get what you want. You might make a fool out of me, and you might fool Margaret, and you are certainly going to fool yourselves, but you won't get what you want. You'll get a lot of trouble, and waste a lot of energy, and every miner's family in every colliery will go into debt, and there will be violence, people will get beaten up, scared, and they'll be hungry, and in the end they'll have nothing to show for it. So unless you're doing it for fun, I'd advise you not to do it at all."

"Well, why don't you give them a little raise," Margaret said, "it wouldn't cost that much, probably less than the strike would cost."

"Listen. Do you think, young lady, that I wouldn't pay my men more money if I could? If it was up to me. I know what it's like working down there. As far as I'm concerned they should be making twice the money and even that wouldn't be enough."

"Well, then. Why don't they get more?"

"It's very complicated. Very complicated. You don't understand what's involved."

"Well, then, Mr. MacDougall. Why don't you explain it to us?" Now Ian was talking. "We're not stupid. Explain it to us. If there is an explanation."

MacDougall looked for a long time at a space over the card table, for a long time. He pursed his lips. He took his left thumb out of his topcoat pocket and put it under his chin.

"Okay," he said, in a soft voice, almost a whisper. "I'll explain it. Listen. This country buys from the United States over 28 million tons of coal which is nearly twice as much as we produce. Why do we do that? Because it's cheaper to buy coal from the States. Why is it cheaper? Because the Canadian government pays buyers in Ontario three dollars a ton to buy American coal. So they don't buy coal from Cape Breton or Nova Scotia, simply because it's cheaper to buy from the States because the taxpayers are paying part of the cost. So we can't sell all the coal we could produce, and what we do sell is under-priced because if we don't sell it cheap they won't buy it. If the federal government would give us the three dollars a ton to sell coal to Ontario and Quebec, then we could afford to pay the extra $2.50 a day the men want. They won't do it. So we don't have the money."

"Is that the whole thing?" Ian said.

"No. That's not the whole thing," MacDougall said. "But it's one thing.... If you are going to have a strike, and you don't want the miners' families to starve, you have to have the backing of the U.M.W., the United Mine Workers of America. Remember that: '...of America.'"

"So what? It's a strong union. They'll back us up. They said so."

"They said so. But they won't. They'll pretend to. But they won't. They'll send encouragement. They'll send some money. But it won't be enough. It won't even be as much as the dues you've been paying them for years."

Ian said. "How can you know that?"

"In the last election in Cape Breton the miners elected a socialist to the federal government." Ian said "So what?" and "It was about time." But he wasn't talking the same as he was when he was sure he was right.

"Let me tell you so what. To an American, a socialist is a communist. Your union is an American union. Your American leader is ambitious. He thinks or at least he knows other people think that the people who voted for a socialist here are communists. He cannot afford to be seen in the States supporting communism. Mark my words, the minute the word communist is used, your American leaders will let go the Cape Breton miners like a red hot poker. And mark my words, the word will be in the newspaper the minute the word strike is used. There will be no money. Or very, very little."

"How do you know all this stuff?" Ian said.

"Because I read," MacDougall said. "It's a spare time activity I recommend. Some people don't care for it. But I find it more useful than drinking rum and playing cards. And more educational. Go down to the little library in the glebe house and see your little priest. He'll tell you exactly what I just told you, because he explained it to me."

"You went to see a priest," Peggy said.

"It's your mother who has problems with priests. I do not believe in priests, or ministers either, so if there is any difference between them, it's not something I'd notice."

"Well I'll be damned," Peggy said.

"I don't think so, Margaret," her father said, "but you'll be wasting your time and energy on a strike. It can't work."

"Have you told us everything?" Neil said.

"If I were you," MacDougall said, "I'd keep my eye on the local union executive. The Americans are not the only ambitious politicians in the labour movement." Neil nodded. I knew he was believing this man. Neil did not want to believe him, but he was having his doubts. Ian too.

"I have one more thing to say, before I leave," MacDougall said. "Margaret."

"Yes, Dada."

"I am not going to fight with you. You'll have to decide for yourself what you'll do. That's what it will be in the end, anyway. I'll tell your mother that tonight. She'll have to accept it. She will accept it when I explain it to her because she won't want to lose you, even for a short time. But she won't like it. You'll have to accept that. Live with it.

"You two men. There are some good jobs coming up. Surface jobs and the pay is good and good chance for advancement. I know this doesn't sound great, and you might not believe me when I say I'm not trying to buy you off the strike, but I do believe you can organize a strike and keep it going quite a while, which is why I would like to have you working for me. But of course if you are involved in the strike, if you are seen as the instigators, I wouldn't have a hope of hiring you on after the strike."

Nobody said a word. We couldn't believe our ears.

"Margaret. I'd like you to walk home with me. You can come right back if you want to. I won't try to talk you into anything or out of anything. I'd just like you to walk home with me."

"Can Ian come and walk me back?"

"Yes. Let him come in fifteen minutes. We'll walk home together, and then he can come and walk you back."

So they left. We're standing there like stumps.

"Do you believe that, Neil ?" Ian said. "Do you think he's right?"

"We'll strike and find out."

"But what do you think, Neil, really?"

"Really? I think he's probably right."

Chapter Six
The Picnic

BY THE TIME of the strike, I was really hoeing into the scribblers. Not a day went by but I was thinking about what I read the night we got back from the beach the day we saw the whale, where Grandfather wrote if Neil and Ian get killed what will the poor girl do, and me the poor girl, it was so spooky, I found, to be reading about yourself what somebody else wrote. I was lucky I was doing it when Grandfather was still around. I would ask him questions about it and he would write down answers, so I filled in a lot of stuff I'd of never known. So I was at it every spare minute. He got a great kick out of it himself. "Ye be the clear Morag yourself," he wrote down once, which I got a big kick out of because by then I'd been all through the stuff she wrote.

Yes, I just about memorized those scribblers. Once I caught on that Da's wasn't the only stuff there, that under his was all Morag's stuff, I couldn't get enough of it. I'd kept up with his because I was always looking at it to see if he wanted anything: "Gimmie the bedpan," or "Get that fella back here and play something." Mostly I'd only look on the page he was on, so if he wrote more than one page I'd likely miss anything ahead of the last page. But sometimes I'd browse back. And when I got way back I caught on Morag started the scribblers long ago and she must of passed them on to Da to keep them going and he did, but not as good as her, hers was almost like something you'd read in a book. Some of them I read over and over again, some I know I memorized it word for word, I read it so often, and that's when it hit me that now it was up to me to keep the scribblers going and write down all the things that happened since my grandfather quit doing it, and even go back and put in stuff I remember that he didn't put, or even stuff he did but I had a different idea of it. I loved doing it. Though I found it hard. It was like Mrs. McGregor said at the wake, having people dead in your family is like carrying a load on your shoulders. It's hard to do but you're glad you're the one that's doing it.

I could rhyme it off for you by heart without a glance

at the scribbler, but I'll read you bits of it, because some of it not everybody would be interested in. And some of it I put it in myself where something seemed to be missing, or if it wouldn't make sense if anybody else read it, like without knowing other stuff that grandfather told me.

She started it out in Gaelic but when she got to the part where she had them talking, herself and Mairi, she shifted to English after the first three things they said. It was "Tha an là blàth an diugh, Morag," and, "Tha, ach bha e fuar gu leòr an dé," and, " Tha, agus fluich." Just weather talk.

Then like it was the next day, she started in again but on the next page and in English, lucky for me: "I decided right then and there I'd write everything down as I remembered it, but in English for fear as Mairi said that soon enough there'll be not a soul in Reserve Mines or anywhere else that would read it in Gaelic.

"When I was thinking of leaving Mabou, I was telling my mother my plans in the kitchen, and she took me by the hand. Without a word she led me out and across the yard to the barn. I didn't know yet, why the barn, and she sat me down on the milking stool and she turned over the milking bucket and sat on it herself, both of us in the empty stall. And she said to me:

"'Okay, Morag. Now tell me again.'

"'I'm going away, is all. That's all there is to it.'

"'There's a lot that go away, Morag, these days. They don't come back.'

"'That's true. Why would they?'

"'I don't want you to go. I'll miss you something awful.'

"'I have to go.'

"'I'll not try to stop you. You're not the kind of person that can be stopped anyway.'

"'There's nothing for me here, Mother.'

"'No, Morag. It's not nothing.'

"'What is it, then?'

"'It's your family. It's the land. It's the music that you love.'

"'But it's not me that'll get the land.'

"'But you could marry into the land. Like I did myself.'

"'And who would I marry? Robert?'

"'Well, you have a good point there.'

"'And the music? Where is it now? They're all gone to work in the Glace Bay mines, the fiddlers, and the pipers, and the dancers, any that can walk at all and sober. They took the music with them. It's with them. It's not with us.'

"'Not all.'

"'Nearly all.'

"'Without the land, the music won't last.'

"'They'll never drop the music, Mother.'

"'They won't drop it. It'll sink away like water in the woods. The music won't be with them long. Go if you think it's right, Morag. But mark my words.'

"'But there's land there too, surely.'

"'Yes. Surely. But who will own it? If you have land, and a house on it, and a barn on it, and cows and chickens and all, nobody can lay you off, and you can always eat, poor as you might be, without getting to your knees for somebody's charity. Go, if you must, Morag, but keep your God, your tongue, your music and get some land.'"

And that is what my grandmother's mother said to her. As a warning.

And wasn't her mother right. Indeed, she did what her mother said. She got the land, and a house on it, built by her husband Donald and his brother Roddie, but she must have been thinking of her mother when she wrote the next thing in her scribbler I'm gonna read you. She was talking to her friend Mairi, telling her about it. She wrote what she said to her.

"I came from milking the other evening and what do I find but the two of them, sitting at the kitchen table, a bottle of rum between them. I stopped and listened at the door and 'Oh,' says Roddie, 'I'll tell you, Donald, a man with a farm has got two jobs. Works all day in the pit, itself more than enough for a strong back, and not home more than a minute but it's out into the field. How could even a strong man keep it up for long?'

"I'll tell you, Mairi, I couldn't believe my ears. And in English, Mairi. In English. Talking in English about how great it is to work in a hole in the ground. As if we didn't agree to get the money to make a go of the farm and be free of the pit so he wouldn't have to work like a worm. I couldn't listen to any more of that.

"I marched in. 'I'll have a drink a that,' I said. I grabbed the bottle. I took it to the bedroom and poured it into the slop pail with the morning piss. And back I went to the kitchen and fired the bottle into the wood box and put the slop pail on the table between them. 'There you are,' I said. 'If you want to make pigs out of yourselves, there's the clear thing.'

"They said nothing. Sat there like two gawks. I went out and pruned my currant bushes till I settled down, then I went to my room and played some miserable laments on my fiddle and went to bed and when he landed in bed he put his hand on me and I let on I was asleep, but he knew I wasn't.

"And you better learn to do it, girl. There's no good talking to them. They think the job is like the land, that it just stays there. But the job is like the music, like mother said, it's like water in the woods. It's there till it's gone. The woods is always there. Cut it down, it grows again. Like grass. Plow it over and next year it's there again. They're too stunned to know that the job is not like that. They show up for work and the washhouse door is locked."

117

She wrote more but that's the best part. She must have been one awful terror. She didn't care what she wrote down. I wanted to do it just like her, if I could be as lively as her, and it was when the strike talk really got going that I got really excited about the scribblers so I was writing everything down.

FOR A WHILE everything with Ian and Neil was the strike and then one day everything wasn't the strike and Ian got up and started packing a picnic basket and I knew right away the way he was doing it it wasn't for the strike at all. It was a good clear cold sunny day and Ian and Neil and Peggy and me we got in the car and drove out of Glace Bay talking about Mabou and seeing the other side of Cape Breton and where my people came from and should we hurry right there or go first around the Cabot Trail and spend just the evening in Mabou and maybe stay with my relatives most of them we had never seen face to face or just have tea and get out of there and not one mention of the strike or coal though all the time it was right there back of us and back of our minds I guess also because the talk was about where I

came from which was of course Mabou where my grandmother came from, though all I knew of it was what I saw
in the notebooks. Which wasn't much. We talked about the
Cabot Trail and which way we should go 'round—and Neil
said before they had decent guardrails people would go
clockwise to be on the inside hugging the mountains all the
way around but that like everything today it was safe now
and you could go either direction, and this time of year
there wouldn't be the tourists. But really we didn't talk
much and maybe we were thinking about the strike and
when we did talk it was about Mabou people who were
mostly farmers and fishermen although they had coal mines
over there. There were families worked there and later came
to Glace Bay because they were experienced miners. But we
thought of them as fishermen and farmers. My people but
with a different life and a different language, which I figured they still talked.

It turned out we looked at everything through the car
windows. We drank from a bottle and drove. We never
went around the Cabot Trail. We drove through Mabou
which is a town and down to the Mabou Harbour and out

to Mabou Coal Mines which aren't coal mines anymore. We thought we'd go somewhere for a meal but ended up eating this and that in the car. And drinking.... We could have stopped for directions to where my relatives were but we didn't want to talk with people and finally saw the house from a distance and we were pretty sure this is the place my people came from, the part of Mabou they thank God called The Coal Mines. But I wasn't going up to the house and Neil acted like he was too drunk to go but it was Ian was drinking the hardest and rubbing his face to keep seeing the road.

And soon it was night and we were really in the country with the houses so far apart from one another and us on the road so far from each one of them, driving along so slow you might say that Ian was walking the car, and probably when he was wiping his face one of the tires caught in the side of the road and he couldn't get it back, just kept on driving, slowly, till the bottom of the car scraped along the edge of the ditch and then the car almost stopped. Then it started sliding. The one tire over the edge and creaking along on the bottom of the car, just kept sliding, everyone quiet, Ian leaning away from the slide with his shoulder out the window. But the back wheel went over the edge very very slowly and we rode down the slanted side of the ditch and settled in the bottom. And Ian decided he had to take a pee but couldn't open his door so Peggy got out her side and Ian scrunched over and out with her and I knew we were in it for the night. Neil was chuckling like a baby chuckling. Ian and Peggy went off with their arms around each other and what was left in the bottle, the two of them heading for the woods to take that pee. And me I had Neil and the wall of a ditch on one side and woods on the other. And later I wrote in the scribbler, "After all day looking and looking there he was my own. I loved Neil. And the whole friggin' Cabot Trail meant nothing to me compared to riding in that car or being anywhere with him. And Neil's big hand where I wanted it and the whole car to ourselves. Looking back is one thing but looking forward who could know I was making love to a man pretty soon dead?"

Chapter Seven

The Glace Bay Miners' Museum

OF COURSE everything MacDougall said came true. Once the strike got going it seemed to drop out of the hands of the miners completely. The big meetings all took place in Montreal. Nobody knew what was going on. There wasn't enough money, we got seven dollars a week to live on. But we didn't have a family to feed, just ourselves. And lucky for us Ian and Neil had a good bootleg pit for the first month, but then they put a stop to that. That was one of the worst things that happened during the strike, and it was the union itself that did it. They didn't want the men selling bootleg coal because they figured if the merchants in Sydney and Glace Bay couldn't get coal to heat their stores they'd put pressure on to end the strike. Neil said that was foolish because there wasn't that much coal mined, it was just a trickle. But it was great because it gave the men something to do and it brought in money, and it kept the schools and churches going and even the homes of miners who hadn't stored up coal in advance.

There were some good things about the strike. Peggy and me really enjoyed going around and talking to the women getting them to support the strike and not to be at their men to get back to work. It got hard as the strike wore on, of course, because people were getting hard up. But we got a lot of tips on how to make cheap meals and we'd write everything down and tell everybody. We even got people going around showing people how to cook and how to sew to save money. We learned a lot.

Another nice thing about the strike was that since nobody was working all the singers and fiddlers and dancers had time on their hands and they'd go around giving free concerts, or they'd charge a little and they'd donate the money to the relief fund. Almost every week, sometimes more often there'd be a show. So that was great.

But when it was all over we were no better off than before. The union made a deal for a dollar a day I think it was. They started out looking for $2.50. But even that didn't amount to anything because they only got the raise if they put out more coal than before the strike, which was nearly impossible.

But the worst of it was, if there hadn't been a strike and MacDougall kept his word Ian and Neil might have been working on the surface and never been in an accident at all, and they'd still be here. As it was, they went back to the pit, and as it was, they got killed. They both got killed the same minute. I was up to Reserve keeping house for my mother when I heard the whistle. I heard the dogs howling for two nights before so soon's I heard the whistle I took off for the pit. They both just were taken up when I got there. They had them in a half-ton truck with blankets over them.

"Take them to Mama's," I said.

"We got to take them to hospital."

"You take them to Mama's, Art. I'll wash them and I'll get them to the hospital."

"Listen, Snooker, the doctor's got to see them."

"I'll call the doctor."

"I can't."

"Listen, you bastard. Whose are they, yours or mine? You haven't even got an ambulance. I'll wash them, and wherever they go, they'll go clean and in a regular ambulance, not your goddamn half broken down truck."

So he took them down to Mama's and they carried them in and put one on Mama's bed and one on the couch in the kitchen. I knew what to get. I saw Charlie Dave keep a dead frog for two years when he was going to school. I went to the Medical Hall and got two gallons. Cost me a lot. I got back as fast as I could. I locked the house before I left so's nobody could get in. Mama was visiting her sister in Bras d'Or and I didn't know when she'd be back.

When I got back, there was a bunch around the door. They started to murmur.

"Fuck off," I said. "I'm busy."

To make matters worse, my grandfather was left alone all that time. He died. Choked. I took his lungs. It wasn't so much the lungs themselves, though, I think they were a good thing to take, though they don't keep too well, especially the condition he was in, as just something to remind me of the doctor who told him he couldn't get compensation because he was fit to work. Then I took Neil's lungs because I thought of them connected to his pipes and they show, compared to grandfather's, what lungs should look like. I was surprised to find people have two lungs. I didn't know that before. Like Neil used to say, look and ye shall see. I took Neil's tongue since he always said he was the only one around still had one. I took his fingers too because he played his pipes with them. I didn't know what to take from Ian so I took his dick since he always said to Neil that was his substitute for religion to keep him from being a pit pony when he wasn't drinking rum or playing forty-fives.

Then my mother came in. She went hysterical and out the door. I had each thing in its own pickle jar. I put them all in the tin suitcase with the scribblers and deck of cards wrapped in wax paper and the half empty quart of black death they left after last Sunday's drinking and arguing. I got on the bus and came home to the Bay and put in the pipes and Neil's missal and whatever pictures were around.

Then I took the trunk to Marie, my friend next door and asked her to put it in her attic till I asked for it. Don't tell anybody about it. Don't open it. Forget about it. Then I came back here and sat down and I thought of something my grandmother used to sing, "There's bread in the cupboard and meat on the shelf, and if you don't eat it, I'll eat it myself." I was hungry.

I knew they'd come and haul me off. So I packed my own suitcase, Neil's really, but mine now. They came with a police car and I didn't give them a chance to even get out of the car. I jumped right into the back seat like it was a taxi I was waiting for. I just sat right in and said, "Sydney River please." Sydney River, if you're not from around here, is the cookie jar where they put rotten tomatoes so they won't spoil in the barrel. So they put me in till they forgot about me; then when they remembered me they forgot what they put me in for. So they let me go.

My mother lived in the house all the time I was away. I told her to, to keep it for me and give her a better place to live. When I got back I told her: "You can stay here and live with me, Mother, if you like."

"Thanks anyway," she said. "But I'm not feeling too good. I think I'll go back to Reserve."

"So stay. I'll look after you."

"Yes, you'll look after me. You'll look after me. And what if I drop dead during the night?"

"If you drop dead during the night, you're dead. Dead in Glace Bay is the same as dead in Reserve."

"Yes. And you'll look after me dead, too, I imagine. You'll look after me. What'll you do? Cut off my tits and put them in bottles."

I said to her, "Mother, your tits don't mean a thing to me."

By then she had her suitcase packed and she left walking. "Have you got everything?" I called.

"If I left anything," she yelled back, "pickle it."

"O.K.," I said. She walked. Then she turned and yelled, "Keep it for a souvenir."

"O.K.," I yelled.

I was sorry after that I said what I said. I wouldn't mind having one of her tits. After all, if it wasn't for them, we'd all die of thirst before we had our chance to get killed.

Marie came over then with the suitcase and we had a cup of tea and she helped me set things up. We had to make shelves for the jars. Everything else can go on tables and chairs or hang on the wall or from the ceiling as you can see. Marie is very artistic, she knows how to put things around. I'm the cook. We give tea and scones free to anyone who comes. You're the first. I guess not too many people know about it yet. A lot of things are not keeping as well as we would like, but it's better than nothing. Perhaps you could give us a copy of your tape when you get it done. That might make a nice item. It's hard to get real good things and you hate to fill up with junk just to have something.

For more Breton Books

see the following pages . . . .

ALSO AVAILABLE FROM
Breton Books & Music

STERLING SILVER
by SILVER DONALD CAMERON
Rants, Raves and Revelations
Essays from over 25 years of writing, never before in print form—*Sterling Silver* demonstrates a wide range of Silver Donald's interests. From suicide to love and fear, craftsmanship and community—this is Silver Donald Cameron angry, hopeful, incisive and amused.
$21.50

CAPE BRETON QUARRY
by STEWART DONOVAN
A book of poetry that gravitates between rural and urban Cape Breton Island, and the experience of working away. Stewart Donovan has written a relaxed, accessible set of poems of a man's growing up and his reflections on the near and distant past of his communities.
A lovely, lasting little book.
$11.00

SILENT OBSERVER
written & illustrated
by CHRISTY MacKINNON
A children's book of emotional & historical substance—autobiographical story of a little girl who lived in rural Cape Breton & in the world of a deaf person.
$21.50

ARCHIE NEIL
by MARY ANNE DUCHARME
From the Life & Stories of Archie Neil Chisholm of Margaree Forks, C. B.
Saddled with polio, pride, and a lack of discipline, Archie Neil lived out the contradictory life of a terrific teacher floundering in alcoholism. This extraordinary book melds oral history, biography and anthology into "the triumph of a life."
$18.50

CAPE BRETON
BOOK OF THE NIGHT
Stories of Tenderness & Terror
51 extraordinary, often chilling, tales, pervaded with a characteristic Cape Breton tenderness—a tough, caring presentation of experience
$16.25

ANOTHER NIGHT
Cape Breton Stories True & Short & Tall
More great storytelling from the pages of *Cape Breton's Magazine.* Some witty, some eerie, some heartrending, these stories convey the pleasure we take in entertaining one another.
$16.25

A FOLK TALE JOURNEY
THROUGH THE MARITIMES
by HELEN CREIGHTON
eds. Michael Taft & Ronald Caplan
72 folk tales from a lifetime of collecting. Dr. Creighton introduces each storyteller, and then lets them talk to us directly, in their own words. A wonderful portrait of the faith and courage of the collector and the trust of the storyteller. This book is a Maritime treasure.
$23.50

DOWN NORTH:
The Original Book of
Cape Breton's Magazine
Word-and-Photo Portrait from the first 5 years of *Cape Breton's Magazine*
239 pages, 286 photographs
$23.50

CAPE BRETON LIVES:
A Second Book from
Cape Breton's Magazine
300 pages of Life Stories • 120 photos
$23.50

• PRICES INCLUDE GST & POSTAGE IN CANADA •

CONTINUED ON NEXT PAGE

ALSO AVAILABLE FROM
Breton Books & Music

WATCHMAN
AGAINST THE WORLD
by FLORA McPHERSON
The Remarkable Journey of Norman
McLeod and his People from Scotland to
Cape Breton Island to New Zealand
A detailed picture of the tyranny and
tenderness with which an absolute leader
won, held and developed a community—
and a story of the desperation, vigour,
and devotion of which the 19th-century
Scottish exiles were capable.
$16.25

THE MOONLIGHT SKATER
by BEATRICE MacNEIL
9 Cape Breton Stories & The Dream
From a mischievous blend of Scottish &
Acadian roots, these stories blossom, or
explode softly, in your life. Plus her
classic play set in rural Cape Breton.
$11.00

ECHOES FROM LABOR'S WARS
by DAWN FRASER
Industrial Cape Breton in the 1920s
Echoes of World War One
Autobiography & Other Writings
Introduction by David Frank
& Don MacGillivray
Dawn Fraser's narrative verse and stories
are a powerful, compelling testament to
courage, peace & community. They be-
long in every home, in every school.
$13.00

THE CAPE BRETON GIANT
by JAMES D. GILLIS
& "Memoir of Gillis" by Thomas Raddall
A book about not one,
but two singular Cape Bretoners.
"Informative, entertaining, outrageous...!"
$10.00

HIGHLAND SETTLER
by CHARLES W. DUNN
A Portrait of the Scottish Gael
in Cape Breton & Eastern Nova Scotia
"This is one of the best books yet written
on the culture of the Gaels of Cape Breton
and one of the few good studies of
a folk-culture."— *Western Folklore.*
$16.25

CAPE BRETON CAPTAIN
by Captain DAVID A. McLEOD
Reminiscences from
50 Years Afloat & Ashore
A rough-and-tumble autobiography of
sailing, shipwreck, mutiny, and love.
$13.00

THE SPECIALINK BOOK
by SHARON HOPE IRWIN
with chapters by Linda Till, Karen
Vander Ven, Dale Borman Fink
SpeciaLink is a national network based in
Cape Breton devoted to getting *all* children with special needs into mainstream
childcare—the real world, rather than
segregated settings. The story of the road
to these principles, and of the symposium
that made them the national agenda.
$18.50

CASTAWAY ON CAPE BRETON
Two Great Shipwreck Narratives
in One Great Book!
1. Ensign Prenties' *Narrative* of Shipwreck at Margaree Harbour, 1780
(Edited with an Historical Setting
and Notes by G. G. Campbell)
2. Samuel Burrows' *Narrative* of Shipwreck on the Cheticamp Coast, 1823
(With Notes on Acadians Who Cared for
the Survivors by Charles D. Roach)
$13.00

• PRICES INCLUDE GST & POSTAGE IN CANADA •